HENRY 3

JOSEPH KRUMGOLD

HENRY 3

DRAWINGS BY ALVIN SMITH

ATHENEUM **1967** NEW YORK

For my father **HENRY**

1

"ALL RIGHT," I TOLD HIM. "I'M A HUNDRED AND FIFTY-four percent." By then, everything hurt. And the only way to keep him from hammering at me, at my ear, at my neck, at the side of my head, was to let him into the biggest secret there is about me.

He stopped hitting me, at least. "You're a hundred and fifty-four percent normal!" He didn't move from where he sat on the top of my chest. But his mouth, open full and pulling for air, turned into a smile. "Where'd you ever get all that I.Q.?"

I found the collar of my T-Shirt where it was ripped and wiped the blood away from under my nose. "It's just the I.Q. I happen to have, that's all, and the thing is," I whispered with what breath I had left, "you won't tell anyone, will you?"

"Why not?" He shifted to the rear and made himself comfortable on my stomach. He seemed to admire the sight of me. "You must be a natural born genius."

"I don't know about that. All I'm asking is for you not to spread it around Crestview, the percent I am."

"Why not?"

I lay there in the drive that led up to the empty school and I rolled my head in the white gravel. There was no way I could tell him, why not. Without going back, way back to the very beginning.

To begin with, I don't come from anywhere. I was born in a lower berth of the Atchison, Topeka and Santa Fe Railroad about an hour outside of Flagstaff, Arizona. Ever since, I've lived outside a half dozen other places all the way from Seattle, Washington, to Easton, Pennsylvania. That was on account of my Dad. He was forever getting a better job somewhere else, with the company he's always worked for.

Wherever we lived I was alone, mostly. That was on account of me. I'm smart. When I read a page in a book I can't forget it. Explain something to me and I catch on quick. I like school. Mostly I'm at the top of my class.

But it's no great help in making friends, moving so much and being smart. The truth is I never did have a best friend except for three weeks once, a kid by the name of Paco Gibson in Berkeley, California. That broke up when I got appointed crossing guard for the fourth grade, which was Paco's job, because I had higher marks.

I couldn't help it. There may be some who can manage how smart they are. Not me. You hear that whiz kids are getting popular and how brains are all the fad now on account of outer space. But it's never worked out for me. No one cheers the A's I get on my report card. Or rushes in to pal with an example, when that's what the teacher points me out to be. Hardly anybody wants to hang out with a guy who keeps showing him up all the time. Maybe it's my fault, the way I handle things.

This time it was going to be different. This time we were going to do something about it, about me. Because Crestview, outside of New York City, was the end of the line for us. Dad was in the Home Office of his company now with a chance to make Vice-President. And Crestview was going to be the first permanent home I ever had, for five years at least. I talked it over with Ma that maybe I'd get along better, now we'd arrived, if I laid off at least being so smart. In school, especially. Ma thought it might help, just to get me started.

That was the idea I had, that first day in Crestview. But it was nothing I could explain to the guy who was sitting on top of me.

He was kept in after class that first day for setting off a paper airplane during social studies. Miss Dokstra, the teacher of the eighth grade, set him to work in the back of the room copying some sentence a hundred and fifty times while she gave me an aptitude test.

That's what usually happens in a new place. They hand you this quiz with boxes and circles and words to fill in. Considering all the different schools I've been in, I'm used to them. I let myself go, since the score you make is private.

Once or twice, when she was marking my test, Miss Dokstra looked up at me with a surprised nod. Tired as she seemed, the way you find most teachers, she had a

5

nice smile with a dimple. By the time she came to the end she was running a pencil through her hair like it was a one tooth comb. "From the records you brought, I expected something special. But this," she said, "this is about as good a performance as we've ever seen in Crestview."

He delivered his sentences just then, this other fellow. Miss Dokstra told him he could leave.

"I really don't think I ought to keep this from you," she turned back when we were alone. "It's against regulations. But the way it scores is one hundred and fifty-four percent." She was as pleased as if I'd been handed to her for a present.

We left the school together and Miss Dokstra promised I was going to find Crestview very enjoyable. I made the remark I certainly hoped so and watched her stoop into her Volkswagen, the only car still in the parking lot.

That's when he showed up again, the one who was in class with us. He came out from behind a corner of the school. I was certainly glad to see him, anyone who'd wait around just for the chance to meet me. But after the remark he'd heard from Miss Dokstra, about my performance, all he wanted to talk about was my I.Q. He was excited to find out how much brighter I was than anyone else in Crestview. What'd I score? That's all he kept asking. I wasn't going to tell him, not when the whole idea was to keep it secret. I tried to get away. He thought I was brushing him off. That's what did it.

I've had my share of fights. My best hold is sort of a half nelson where you get a guy's arm behind his back. Once you do you can force it up to his neck and practically wreck him. I couldn't even find this one's arm to grab onto, the size of him and the speed he had and the power.

And that's how I came to be dug into the sharp white pebbles of the driveway with him on top asking me, why not?

"For the simple reason," I told him, "it'll ruin me here if anyone finds out."

"I wouldn't say that. Myself, I'm really glad to meet you." Whenever he moved, it felt as though my ribs were caving in. "I'm Fletcher Larkin." He put out his hand. I thought it was to help me up. But after a couple of shakes he sat where he was. "How about you?"

"I'd just as soon get up."

"I mean your name."

I twisted away from the rock that was wedged into my back. "Henry."

"Henry what?"

"Henry Three."

"What kind of last name is that?"

At least he was being sociable. No matter how I felt, my left shoulder, and the bruise on my knee, and the weight in my jaw, the best thing was to get on the right side of Fletcher Larkin. Maybe he was someone who'd keep a secret. "It isn't any last name," I explained. "It's just that my grandfather was Henry. And Dad, he's Henry Lovering, Junior. I'm Henry Three."

"Henry Third, you mean."

"Not me. Henry Third's some character out of Shakespeare or he's a king with a beard. It gives you the wrong idea. I don't want to spread the notion I'm proud of myself. Three's good enough. With the American number." I wrote it in the air. "Henry 3."

"Then all I want to tell you, Henry Three, is that I'm sorry I slugged you." He swung off me and sat on his heels in the lawn that bordered the drive. "It's only that I couldn't let you walk out on me. Not the first day you show up here. You don't know me well enough for that."

With the weight of him gone, big as he was, everything was a lot easier except to understand Fletcher Larkin. "How long does someone have to know you, I mean before they walk out on you?"

"Well, it depends," Fletcher said, "on the individual. But with your I.Q. it shouldn't be too long, you know, before you size things up. I give you a couple of days, maybe, before you never want to see me again."

"Maybe you're wrong." I sat up in the gravel and spoke to him as sincerely as I could. "As long as you're sorry about what happened, I certainly don't want to be the one to keep up any hard feelings. You're the first guy I've met in Crestview, I mean to have anything to do with. And far as I'm concerned, I came here wanting to be friendly."

I don't know why Larkin thought that was so funny, the laugh it gave him. "Not with me?"

"I wouldn't say that?"

"You don't even know me."

"Well, aside from the beating you handed out, you seem all right. Offhand, I'd say you looked fine."

"Me?" Fletcher asked. He searched around till he found a blade of grass that suited him and he chewed on it, studying me. "You know, maybe you are different, Henry Three. Maybe with you, it could work out."

"What?"

"Well, you mentioned being friendly."

8

"I wouldn't like anything better."

Fletcher shook his head in surprise. "You're the only one I ever had a battle with who took it that way. And when you consider this is the second year I've put in with Dokstra, in the eighth grade," he blew out the piece of grass, "it might be a good idea if, you know, I did team up with a brain. So it's fine with me, too, Henry Three."

"Well, good." The way it hurt all over, that didn't matter anymore, long as there was the chance of keeping the truth about me quiet. I crawled out of the gravel and sat where it was softer, at least, on the grass. "Is there anything I can do for you?" I asked Larkin.

"No." It startled him, the question did. "Not that I can think of."

"Well, if there's anything you ever need that I can lend you a hand with, just let me know."

"Thanks."

"Me, though, long as we're being friendly, I had in mind to ask you to keep quiet about my percent. Just not to mention it."

"Where'd be the fun of that?" Fletcher asked. "I mean that was the thought I had when I heard Dokstra talking to you. I couldn't help think of the shock you were going to hand this crowd, the kids they got running around here."

"You're not going to tell them?"

"Sure I am. First thing tomorrow morning. Wait'll you see their faces!" Larkin went pop-eyed to give me the effect.

"You can't!" I told him.

"I sure can."

"Not if we're going to be friendly."

"Just a second." Larkin came to one knee and rubbed a hand around the back of his neck. "Is that what it depends on? Me promising you that I'll shut up?"

"Well, sort of. That's what I had in mind."

"Then we're quits." Fletch came to his feet. He looked around and went to pick up his books that lay in the gravel road. "I don't know what kind of a guy you are. Right off, you seem a lot different from the rest of the bunch here in Crestview. But me, I don't shut up about anything.

And I don't give promises just to make a friend. So the both of us, Henry Three, we're quits."

"Then all I'm asking you, Larkin, is to do me a favor. Do you have to tell them?"

"No." He kept from starting down the driveway. "I don't see why you're so Federal dead set against anyone hearing your percent. If it was me, with any kind of an I.Q. like that, brother! I'd put it out over Channel Five. But if that's the way you feel about it," he shrugged, "I don't have to tell them. I don't have to do anything. I'm just not making any promises."

"Look, Larkin," I stopped him for just another second. "Please."

"It was good to meet you, Henry Three." Fletcher swung one finger at me. "I'll be seeing you around."

I watched the square back of him going away, down the road that led to the street below. He turned light and then dark through the late afternoon shadows of the trees along the block. Then he turned a corner and was gone, Fletcher Larkin, some guy I never knew before, who all of a sudden my whole future depended on.

2

IT WAS BAD. WHEN I SAW MYSELF IN THE WINDOWS OF THE
school, and it was all windows same as a supermarket, with
wide overhanging roofs, I didn't know how I was going to
get home. I looked like something out of Southeast Asia
getting evacuated, on the seven o'clock news, to government
held territory near the capital. There was a rip in my shorts
that traveled to my belt almost. And blood, starting to
dry. And eight blocks for me to go, me, the new boy in
town passing all those fine houses, looking a wreck.

I thought to wait until dark. The only water around was
in a little fountain that stood in the school patio. I washed
what I could and stood there to dry. From the small hill
the school was on you could see the faraway buildings of
New York City, with the burn of the setting sun lighting
up one and then the other.

I picked out where my Dad had his office, the Empire State Building. I recognized it from the picture there is on his letterhead, the one Dad had for business, and now there it stood for real, the highest building in the world. There might be newer skyscrapers in New York and fancier but the Empire State was practically a trademark for my Dad's company just because it was old and it still looked down on all the others. And for us, for our family, it was the end. Here's where we always aimed to live, at the foot of the Empire State Building with my Dad in his own Home Office.

The sun went. New York City reached up high as a range of far off mountains. The office lights coming on made you think of hill towns, way up, getting ready for the night. Except all those offices up there were the most important in the world, from what I heard. They were for the biggest executives of the best companies. And now that my Dad had one for himself there was a chance for me, even. Some day I'd make it up there too, where all you had to push was a buzzer to get whatever you wanted sent in.

That was for someday. All I had in mind right now was to end up the personal friend of whoever might be interested. If only it was all right with him, with Fletcher Larkin. According to the way he felt, by morning the whole of Crestview would know all about me.

To make things worse, I found out that Fletcher belonged to the oldest family in town. A cab driver told me. It was a taxi passing the school on its way back to the railroad station that gave me the chance to get home without waiting for dark. When the driver saw the shape I was in and

heard it was my first day in town, he tried to sympathize.

"Whatever you got hit with," he twisted to look me over, "don't get this place wrong, young fellow. You've come to the finest, executive-type development in the New York

City area." He described how well-off everyone was, with most up to Chryslers and Buicks plus some Cadillacs sprinkled in. And how there were fourteen different style houses to choose from, so hardly any two looked alike. And each one, the last word modern.

"Except for The Mansion of course," mentioned the driver. "That's where the Larkins live. They're like the aristocrats of the place. This whole country around here used to be called Larkin's Meadows."

I didn't hear much else. It was enough to think over, how I was quits with the most important kid, it looked like, in Crestview."

My big sister spotted us through one of the uncurtained windows as we pulled into our driveway. She was waiting for me in the kitchen, her hair done in curlers so she looked like a T.V. antenna. At the shock I was her face fell open and she moaned. The way she rushed to help me through the door, I got caught in the wires of her hairdo, trying to explain that it wasn't a car that ran me over.

She let go and stepped back to sit on a case that was half unpacked with pots and pans. "You had a fight?" she moaned even louder. "On our first day here?"

Sis was joined by Lady, our three-year-old. At the sight of me, the way I was, and Sis, collapsed, Lady took off in a jet-powered scream.

"The taxi," I tried to get across. "He's waiting, Sis. Can you get me a dollar?"

"One, two, three," yelled Lady who was learning to count.

"Whatever's wrong?" I heard my mother. She looked in from the dining room and her eyes went wide. "Henry!"

She was very quiet.

"It's the taxi outside."

Ma picked up her purse from the crowded kitchen table and disappeared. Once the taxi shifted into gear and pulled out, she was back in the kitchen door and she stared. "That'll do, Margaret," she tapped my sister quiet.

"But we're hardly even moved in yet," wailed Sis. "And look at him."

"That's what I intend to do." With a hand on my neck, Ma led me to the sink. "Please," she asked Sis, "my overnight bag in the bedroom. And you'd better ask Agnes to start cleaning down in the playroom." Agnes was the new maid who showed up that morning. "No use letting her in on this, whatever this is. And on the piano," Sis looked back from the dining room, "you'll find a pile of fresh towels." That left only Lady. "Hush sweet," mother clucked at her. "Say four, five, six."

Lady played it safe. "One, two, three."

Ma switched on the light over the sink. She studied me and touched her cheek to my forehead. I felt a kiss on the scratch next to my right eye. "Henry Three," she asked, "how's the best fellow I ever had?"

"There was this kid, that's all. He was waiting for me after school and what happened — ."

"No talk." Ma had the water running. "It's all over." She ripped the cellophane off a new blue dish cloth. "Breathe deep. It's all easy now, easy."

It felt good, the spongy cloth, almost steaming, across my eyes and down around the back of my neck. Ma tipped my head over until it was under the warm water and her fingers went searching, strong and sure, through my hair and around my ears for where it hurt. She shoved the stool in behind me and I hoisted onto it leaning over the sink afraid, now I wasn't alone anymore, that I couldn't catch my breath fast enough to keep from letting go.

The towels Sis brought were like crawling into bed, the fresh smell of them covering me soft and dark as a blanket, working on my shoulders and down my back as the hands kept moving to just the right places. Ma let my head through and pulled the towel around my neck. "Hold tight!" She screwed the top off a tiny brown bottle and dipped the glass rod it had.

The worst place it hurt was under one ear and the scrape on my elbow. Ma took a package of bandaids and, carefully, she went to work on me as if I were a stamp album. "Except for a Purple Heart," she finished with my face in both her hands, "that just about does it, until we get you into a good hot bath." She wiped her own hands on a towel. "How about now?" she asked me. "Would it make you feel any better to talk about it now?"

"It wasn't my fault," I started out.

"Of course it was, son." Ma brushed the wet hair back along the side of my head. "That's not what I'm interested in, for the moment. But just in passing, Henry child, whatever happened was your fault."

"But you don't know, Ma."

"The facts seem clear," Ma smiled at me. "You weren't clever enough to sidestep this battle. That's obvious. Or good enough, by the look of you, to win it." Ma finished smoothing my hair. "None of us was going to make that kind of a mistake in Crestview. Remember?"

I remembered. It was back in our old house outside

Easton, Pennsylvania. It was after the furniture vans had pulled out on their way to Crestview. The house was empty and we sat on the stairs of the still hall, my mother, Sis, Lady and I, and Ma gave us her word that this was the last time we'd ever move so far from where we lived. My mother's never cried, that I know, but that afternoon her eyes were shinier than I'd ever seen as she apologized, to the three of us, for keeping us homeless.

She was sorry for us, Ma was, because we'd never come to know any real security. There was never a home she fixed for the family that couldn't be broken up by a telephone call from Dad's office. There was only one place we'd ever be safe, Ma described, and that was at the top. Once we were up there, we'd really be secure. We'd decide about ourselves, then, and no one ever after would have a chance to interfere.

"That's what we're reaching for in Crestview," Ma told us, "for the very top. This is the chance your Dad's been working for all your lives. But it isn't only him, getting up there. Crestview's a job for each one of us. Not nine to five, but all around the clock. Not a job to work at, but one we all have to live."

Because Crestview, Ma explained, was the people who could help us reach where we wanted to go. Our neighbors were the ones Dad did business with, who had the influence and the power to see him make good. And it was up to us to get along with them, even if we had to bend over backwards. If we didn't, Ma and all of us agreed, if we failed, then it was going to be no one's fault but our own.

"But I couldn't bend over more backwards," I tried to explain about Fletcher Larkin, "without breaking in two."

Except I didn't mention my own private worry, where I let out my percentage, I told Ma everything just the way it happened.

"Congratulations," said Ma.

"For what?"

"For the exam. That's your best mark yet."

"Congratulations?" asked Sis. Now she knew what was wrong with the telephone. She hadn't had one call, late as it was, even though she'd put in a full day at high school meeting a dozen different fellows. Usually, Sis does a lot better than that. "No wonder," she complained. "With us feuding against the top family in town. What are we going to do about it, Ma?"

"We're going to make up with the Larkins." Ma went to the phone. "Soon as I find out something about them." Ma tried to talk with a lady she'd met at the supermarket, a Mrs. Lathrop, who turned out to be not at home. And then we came to know as much about the Larkins as we thought we'd ever need.

Sis answered the four tones at the front door to find a little man with a black hat and a mustache who didn't have anything to say. He handed Sis a wad of paper, tipped his hat and left.

"It looks legal," Sis hurried into the kitchen. Under the sink light, Ma unfolded the papers in their blue cover. As she turned the long pages, slower and slower, she seemed to wilt. She half hoisted herself onto the sink, for support maybe, and when she looked up to where we waited Ma was a little pale. "One thing seems very definite," she spoke mostly to herself. "Mr. Larkin does not want to make up with the likes of us."

"That's from Fletcher Larkin's father?" I asked.

"It's a subpoena. Like a summons. It means you have to go to court."

"Me? He can't be bringing the police into this. They'd have to be on my side! I wasn't the one who started the fight."

"There's no police. This isn't about the fight. Not directly. It's more serious than that." Ma folded the papers. "Mr. Larkin wants to move us out of Crestview."

The noises that came out of Sis you don't get to hear, as a usual thing, outside of a hospital.

I couldn't believe it, the things Ma told us. Mr. Larkin claimed we didn't own the house we bought. That was impossible, Ma knew. But Larkin was ready to take us to court and spend a lot of money trying to prove it. More money than we could afford if we tried to stop him. That way maybe, he could move us out of Crestview if he wanted to.

"But why would he want to?" I climbed off my stool.

"I imagine that's where your fight comes in. We believe you, Henry, all you've told us," Ma touched me under the chin, "without question. But it appears as though young Larkin has reported his own version of your war and he's apparently done it up," Ma sighed and felt across her forehead, "in wide screen and Technicolor. Enough, to send his father into enough of a rage that he wants to see the last of us."

"But that's impossible." The worst Larkin had in mind was to spread my percent all over the place. That was bad enough. For me to end up in Crestview same as everywhere else in the United States, alone. But at least that'd be me, my lookout. Not my family. There was no call for Larkin to get that sore, to kick all of us out of Crestview after only one day. "It doesn't make sense, Ma." I pounded the sink. "I don't understand."

"Neither do I." Ma wrapped the towel around me again. "But quiet, Henry. First thing in the morning, we'll dig into this. We'll find out, get some idea what can be done. The big worry, though, is your father." Ma picked up Lady and hugged her. "With all he's up against at the office, he doesn't need this kind of a load falling on him. Until we see where we're going, he's the one we have to protect. So we're not going to talk about this in front of your father, do you understand?"

"We can explain Henry fell off the garage roof," said Sis.

"There's no way up there," I pointed out. "The back fence is better."

"Whatever you please," Ma begged. "But we're very happy in Crestview, as far as your Dad is concerned. We're doing fine here."

Bewildered as I was, I did my best when the roar of Dad's car came up the driveway. He arrives home from the station the same way every night. Once he puts down his dispatch case, he and Ma hold on to each other for a long time. Then they kiss.

Lady charged into them. "Daddy! One, two, three, four."

"Baby girl!" Dad lifted her high. "You're getting to sound like a computer." He winked at the large smiles we had, Sis and I. "How're things?"

"It was just I was climbing the fence out back," I tried to tell him, but he didn't notice my appearance.

"Seems like home already," Dad lead the way out of

the kitchen, carrying Lady on his shoulders.

I kept to myself all through dinner, trying to puzzle some reason for the sudden fix we were in. I guess it had to be me who was to blame, though I couldn't see how. Thank heavens, Dad had lots to talk about, describing a meeting at A. L. & L.

That's short for the company he's always worked for. It's American Lock and Locomotive, though the company doesn't make locks anymore or even, I don't think, locomotives. What they do make is just about everything else from thumb tacks to intercontinental ballistic missiles in factories that are all over the world. Dad went on about some reorganization plan he was asked to help with, which he judged was a fine opportunity toward making Vice-President.

Thinking back in my own mind to the time we lived outside Santa Fe, New Mexico and Detroit, Michigan, I could see where I never did learn much about getting along with people. But I never did this bad. Where they took it out on my family, what they thought about me. The final jolt was that it had to happen in Crestview, the most important place of all.

"Crestview's perfect," said Dad. "According to Matthews." Mr. John F. Matthews was the actual President of the whole American Lock and Locomotive Corporation. Dad mentioned the quick talk he'd had with Matthews after their meeting broke up. "It wasn't what he said," Dad told us. "But his attitude suggested we'd found just the right background, that Crestview gave us the perfect image for the bracket I'm in at A. L. & L."

I jabbed a piece of corned beef at the thought of Dad

finding out that we weren't living in Crestview anymore. On account of me. I guess I wasn't looking too happy. Nor Ma and Sis either, from the way Dad studied us around the table. "What's wrong?" he asked. "Don't we all like it here in Crestview?" He rubbed the side of his eye to show where I had a bandaid stuck on. "What's wrong with you?"

"Oh that," I swallowed the corned beef. "I tried to tell you about that. You know the fence out back?"

Dad nodded. "Where we had the painters in this morning?"

I'd forgotten. It was a split willow fence Ma wanted white. I couldn't go on with any story about a fresh painted fence. "There was this tree," I started all over again.

"Where?"

"Down near the school," I told him.

"What's that got to do with the fence?"

"What fence?"

"The one out back."

"That got painted today?"

"Yes," said Dad.

"What about it?" I sliced another forkful of corned beef.

"What about what?" Dad pointed his napkin. "You're the one started this."

Ma leaned her face in her hands. "Give up, Henry Three. It's no use."

"Okay?" Dad asked her "What happens here, Ma?"

It was the telephone that saved us. It was Mrs. Lathrop answering Ma's call. Everything at the table stopped, except Lady who was giving herself a facial with the mayonnaise. And then Ma hung up and she stood in the door and it was like the sun changed its mind, with the night coming

23

on, and was flooding back into the dining room again.

Just to meet Ma, you can see where Sis gets her looks. But when she's happy, Ma's really beautiful. Not the way you see on T.V. or in the magazines, not just to look at. She's beautiful the way it can cool up late on a summer afternoon and that's the feeling you get at the sight of her. When she's happy Ma has a laugh like the sprinkle of a hose on a window pane. That's the way it was now, with Ma standing in the kitchen door.

I knew something was wonderful. "What is it?" I yelled.

"Henry, am I ever sorry!" Ma circled the table and the smell of her was everywhere as she took me in her arms. "It wasn't you at all. Can you ever forgive me? I'm an idiot."

"Since when?"

"The way I panicked when those papers showed up. If I'd stopped a moment to think, we'd have known that none of this had anything to do with you. No document like that could be drawn up so fast. And get rushed over here so quick."

Dad sounded like a dropped light bulb. "What document?"

"The one that's moving us out of Crestview," I said.

"No Henry." Ma let me go. "No one's moving. Mrs. Lathrop cleared the whole thing up. The scare we had was over nothing," Ma went weak from laughing, "nothing at all."

"What's nothing?" It was fine the way Dad controlled his speaking voice. "What's all this about fences and trees and documents? What's happening here?"

"Look," said Ma. But when she brought him the legal

paper, that's all the answer Dad needed. He knew all about it. He already knew! And he agreed with Ma, it had nothing to do with us. All it turned out to be was an old law suit Mr. Larkin had against the people who bought his property, the Crestview Land Corporation. They were supposed to use Larkin's Meadow for a farm, not to build a suburb. So Larkin took them to court. And everyone who showed up in Crestview was brought into the case.

"We're involved only technically," Dad said. "We're guaranteed against any loss."

It was the very same thing Ma had heard over the phone from Mrs. Lathrop. And it was only because Dad thought the papers would be coming to his office that he'd never bothered to tell us.

"Bother to tell us!" The way the words came out, you couldn't decide whether Ma was laughing or crying. "We had the idea that us Loverings were the only ones Larkin was gunning for."

"On account of me," I yelled.

"The fight he was in," squealed Sis.

"So it wasn't a tree," Dad put his napkin on the table. "It wasn't a fence. It was a fight."

Mrs. Lathrop told me all about that, too." Ma went on. "Henry couldn't help it."

Was I ever surprised. "How did she know?" I shouted at Ma.

"Fletcher Larkin beats up every new kid who comes to town." Ma passed on Mrs. Lathrop's exact own words. "It's being going on for years."

I felt the grin on my face go stiff. There were no aches left in me, and no puzzle. Nothing was on account of me.

Not the paper. Everybody had one. Not the fight. Everybody had one of those too. "I'm not even to blame that we're feuding with the top family in Crestview," I pointed out.

"They're far from that," Dad explained. No one had anything to do with the Larkins, from all Dad heard. And it wasn't only because of the law suit. "They're the outsiders here, outside the pattern. They don't belong."

And all the while I thought it was me, who didn't belong. I sat back and let everyone apologize for thinking it was on account of me. I laughed with Dad and Ma and Sis while they told me I could forget Fletcher Larkin, that I didn't have to worry about him anymore, that I could cross Fletcher Larkin off my list. I almost got to believing what they said.

When the four tones of the front door sounded again. It was Fletcher Larkin.

3

AND THEN I REMEMBERED HE WAS STILL THE ONE IT depended on, whether all of them in Crestview would know my percentage in the morning. Fletcher Larkin was no one I could stop worrying about.

The whole family came with me to the front door to have a look at him. But aside from "Good evening," there wasn't much that anyone had to say.

Fletcher Larkin stood on the outside mat holding three books and he smiled at each of us. "I get the feeling," he said, "that Mr. Feeny was here. You know, with a black hat."

"He was here," said Sis.

"Maybe I ought to apologize about Mr. Feeny," said Fletch. "I don't know why everyone gets riled when he shows up. That paper, there's nothing personal to it. I mean to get sore about."

"Thank you, Fletcher Larkin," Ma's laugh was pleasant as could be. "I don't think any of us are sore, particularly. Except maybe Henry, here and there."

"You're looking a lot better," Fletch told me.

"I feel all right."

"I figured you would," said Fletch. "So what I thought, the reason I came over, I thought we could do some homework together."

"Homework?" The whole family waited for me to answer. I looked at the ceiling for a while. "Well, why not?"

"How's that?" Dad was startled as the rest of them. "I didn't think you two got along that well, to be doing homework together."

"You don't have to get along so well. Not for homework," suggested Fletch. "The whole thing's down there in the book for you to follow."

"No doubt about that," I explained to the family. "And homework, it has to get done somehow."

Dad and Sis and Ma stared at me as if I were feverish.

"It's a lot better when two go at it," Fletch described. "That way you can lend me a hand, Henry Three, the way you mentioned. And I can help you." Fletcher's eyes opened wide at me. "If you think there's any way I can help you."

"There certainly is," I smiled at him. "You could be a big help."

"For a couple of guys who spent the afternoon taking each other apart," Dad marveled. "What's going on here?"

Ma took the open door from Sis. "It was nice of you to call," she told Fletcher. "But Henry's tied up. I'm afraid we haven't finished our dinner yet. Maybe some other time."

28

"I'm sorry!" said Fletch. "I didn't mean to break in on your dinner, ma'm. I'll just get back to The Mansion and get started on my own. And then maybe," he nodded at me, "I'll be seeing you some other time. Like later."

"Henry," Dad turned me around as the door closed. "I know you took a trouncing from Larkin. He's bigger than you are. But you can't chicken out like that. You can't go around being afraid he'll beat you up again."

"That's not what I'm afraid of."

But back at the dinner table Dad talked to me about courage, and how different men behaved when my father was in the Marines. There was no way he could get the real point, of course. Fletcher Larkin's message came through loud for me, and clear. If I didn't get over to The Mansion and look into the question of homework, there wouldn't be any secret left about me, come morning.

The fact is I needed some glue. And after dinner that's what I yelled through the house as I took off for the garage to get my bike.

I followed the curving sidewalks through the cool night that smelled damp here and there from the sprinklers that were still on. The lawns were dead black pools, straight and regular, with the shrubs in back lighted like scenery on a stage. It was the time of night for *Wagons West*, and you could see the show through the windows of almost every house that you passed.

I stopped at the end of our block to see how Sheriff Bud MacAllister was making out in the big fight that finishes the program every week. When I heard the zing of a bike bell and the growl of a front wheel siren, and two kids coming around the corner almost piled into me. One I recognized from class.

"Hey, it's you," he said. "Lovering." He told the other. "My mother got it over the phone from Mrs. Lathrop. The first day here, he gets waded into by Fletcher Larkin."

"I heard about that," said the second one. "From my sister."

There wasn't any chance for news to get stale in Crestview, from the way it looked.

"Brutal, wasn't it?" asked the first kid whose name turned out to be Gardner Klein.

"It wasn't so bad."

That started them laughing but it didn't seem to be me they were laughing at, so I joined in. "You're lucky you're walking. You should've seen what he did to Chuck, here, Chuck Driscoll."

"Two days in bed," Chuck Driscoll sounded proud. "They gave me penicillin."

As long as that was the deal, to show the punishment you took from Larkin, I pointed out my bandaids. They went over pretty good.

"You've had it," Gardner decided. "You're no different from the rest of us."

That sounded promising. And then they seemed to expect me to ride along with them. So I did. "He won't bother you any more, Fletcher Larkin," I was told by Chuck Driscoll. "And for sure, no one has anything to do with him."

"After a while you hardly even notice he's around," Gardner added. "Larkin never shows up where the rest of us are. For instance," we took a turn in the road that led us out onto the highway, "here."

I hadn't seen it before. Everywhere we lived there was a shopping center. But nothing like The Marketplace they had in Crestview. This was a three sided city practically, all glass and aluminum, with department stores from New York, Macy's and Saks Fifth Avenue, along with auto showrooms and banks, home construction, furniture and even a dealer who sold boats, big ones. And from the look of what went on, you'd think the place was built special for kids.

It was mobbed. There were ten acres of flat cement for parking with not a car on it, because nothing was open except the drug store at one end. Instead there were kids, dozens of them on wheels, on skates and scooters and skateboards, bikes and three-wheelers, homemade pushmobiles and go-carts with pedals and those with motors. There were even a couple of electric jobs, miniature cars that operated off storage batteries. You couldn't ask for a better layout, all those flat empty acres, to let go on.

It was daylight practically, the way the place was lit. Not by the lamps of the parking lot. They were turned off. The light came from the advertisements, long streamers of neon big as clouds, solid cliffs of electric bulbs, and the steady flashing of the high billboards turned the place from red to green to blue.

"You want something at Pirelli's?" Gardned pointed to the drugstore.

"Glue," I told him.

"I mean to drink," he explained. "I'm buying."

"Well, sure." I thanked him. "That'd be fine."

We headed through all the screaming and yelling. Most of those around were playing *Wagons West* because they'd just been looking at it. But you heard lots doing *Crime Doesn't Pay* and *Dead On Arrival*. In the light of all the advertising, 4¼% INTEREST, A MAN'S SMOKE, YOUR DREAM BRA and BEER AT ITS MOST, you never saw such a collection of happy kids.

Here's where I'd be ending up every night, Chuck Driscoll promised me, as we racked our bikes in front of the drug store. Inside, Pirelli's Pharmacy was big as any I'd run into. Like it had a Nursery Department, which they don't have in the usual pharmacy, stocked with seeds, fertilizer and garden tools. I got my glue in Office Equipment, and made it into a booth with Chuck and Gardner over at the fountain.

I was amazed, the number of kids who shoved in after us. The way the talk developed you couldn't help but get the impression they were interested in who I was. They'd all heard about my battle with Fletcher. It gave us something in common at least. I got to be almost thankful to Fletcher for landing on me.

The truth is I never had as good a welcome any place. And certainly never from a higher level bunch of guys who didn't think anymore of treating you to a sixty-five-cent sundae than to a coke. And for all the conversation you heard about cabin cruisers and swimming pools, some of them heated, they behaved plain and ordinary as any gang you'd want to meet. It didn't seem any one of them would be hard to get along with. Or too hard, even, to make friends with according to how things worked out. What that depended on, of course, was Fletcher Larkin.

And each one told me the same thing, Larkin was poison. It was worth your reputation even to be seen talking with

Fletcher Larkin. That didn't make it easier. How could I get a guy to keep a secret for me without talking to him now and then?

I thanked Gardner for his drink and shoved out of the booth. Everyone promised to see me in the morning and it looked as if they actually meant it. Crestview was turning out to be even nicer than I expected. If I could only find out some way to handle Larkin without having anything to do with him.

The kind of house it was, I managed to recognize The Mansion pretty easy. Under the full moon Larkin's home proved to be a clapboard castle that looked like somebody couldn't get their mind made up. There were bits and pieces all over the place that had nothing to do with each other, porches here and balconies there, and a turret that started

out to be a tower and then just quit. Behind the white picket fence, the house stood tall and black in the clear, silver night but taller still was the oak tree out front that spread high over the ridges of the roof.

The only light downstairs came from a side entrance that you reached over a flagstone walk with grass growing through it. The Larkins had to be the only people in Crestview with any grass more than a quarter inch tall and most of the bushes, as well, seemed in business for themselves.

There was a knob you pulled that set a bell ringing and someone pounded down the stairs. The door opened and he stood looking at me with a big, wrap-around smile. "What took you so long?" Fletcher asked me.

"I had to get glue," I explained. "But what's this you've been hinting in connection with homework?"

"Well, the thing is, take you for instance. How old are you?"

"Almost thirteen. I'll be thirteen this Friday."

"There's the difference. I'm going for fourteen. And I'd just as soon get out of the eighth grade this time. I thought working with someone like you, that'd cinch it. So I got to figuring."

"What about?"

"Remember where you mentioned this afternoon how we might get to be friendly? You know, if I didn't let out the score you made."

"Well, look." With my toe I shifted a leaf on the porch. "Friendly could be a little hard to manage. That's not the way it happens here, is it? I mean between you and the rest of them, it seems to me, things aren't so good."

"So good!" The laugh came from Fletch, he had to close

the door to shut the noise out of the house. "I'm poison around here."

"That's the impression I gathered."

"I figured you would, pretty quick. They all know what I think of them." Fletch leaned against the rail. "And now, I guess you know what they think of me. Maybe you even agree with them."

"No. That's not it. Not at all. It's just that I like it here in Crestview, everyone I've met so far. I'd like to get along with everybody, you know, far as I can."

"Then, Henry Three, let me give you a tip. You'd better not hang around me." Fletcher's laugh came back. "That'd kill you a lot faster than that percentage you're worried about."

"Well, exactly." It was startling to find that Larkin's attitude could be so reasonable. "That's why it'd be hard to manage, I mean, for us to be friends."

"Who was bringing that up?"

"You were, weren't you?"

"Not me, I wasn't. I only wanted to mention the suggestion you made this afternoon, when I told you I didn't give promises just to make a friend. But I'm ready to make a deal with you, Henry Three. A straight trade, without any question of friends."

"That's certainly possible. What kind of a deal?"

"Where if we did some homework together, then I'd keep quiet about you. Nothing else. I don't see why I'd even want to mention your name otherwise."

"I'm glad to hear that," I told him. "Along those lines sounds good."

"Except for studying here a couple of times a week, I'd

just as soon never talk to you."

"You mean it?"

"Why not? There'd be no reason, far as I'm concerned, for even noticing you were around."

"That's fine."

"Long as we get set about the homework, whatever happens to you is no interest to me. I couldn't care less."

I took a deep breath. "Well, all I can say Fletcher Larkin, I admire your point of view. It couldn't be better," I told him. "And I promise you, you've got a deal. I'll do my best if you'll do yours." I never imagined my problem in Crestview could get fixed so simple. It was a pleasure to work things out with anyone so straightforward as Larkin. "I sure want to thank you," I said.

"For what?" he opened the door to let me pass. "For not making friends with you?"

"Well, yes," I told him.

Fletch led me into a long room that could've been on T.V. for a Civil War program. And the oldest thing about it was all the books it had. They ran up three of the high walls, stacked behind glass in cases that were carved big and solid as a safe. The place smelled sweet and leathery, like a football that's seen a lot of wear.

"They're the Old Man's," Fletch explained. "The books are."

"You'd think your father was a professor."

"I don't have a father. The Old Man's my Grandpa." We stood at a table with a green cloth top that ran half the length of the room, lit by a hanging lamp that was all different colored glass. Fletcher told me what happened to his father and mother. They were killed in an automobile accident when he was four. That left only Fletcher and his Grandfather and a fellow from Puerto Rico, named Louie Gamero, who did the cooking and took care of things.

"That's why Grandpa had to sell out," Fletcher took out his books. "This was too big a spread for him to handle on his own, almost eight hundred acres in potatoes. Not at his age."

They'd been growing potatoes for the last three hundred years, the Larkins, ever since the family first came to Long Island. It was the first Larkin who showed up, Fletch described, who planted the big tree out front.

"The least Grandpa wanted was for someone else to keep the place up, in potatoes." Fletch found pads and pencils in the big desk behind him. "That's the reason he started sueing the gang he sold to, when they put in their development. The Old Man would just as soon see everyone moved out of here. I don't blame him. What's the use of all the work went into Larkin's Meadows if all you got left is some grass you can't walk on?"

"I don't know." I tried to show him I was interested. "I don't know much about potatoes. But I guess I can see why you light into everybody, if you want them to move."

That's not it." Fletch looked up from trying to find our place in the math book and his smile went wide. "It's just I know what to expect. Everyone who moves in is going to give me the brush anyway, just as soon as Mr. Feeny shows up. So I get to them first. To give them a good personal reason," Fletch laughed, "why they ought to lay off me." He went back to turning pages. "No one needs them. Except for you. You're a brain." He pulled out a chair for me to sit down. "At least, you got something worth trading for."

"Well," I gave him the promise. "I'll do my best."

We worked together on math, not the homework we had but the next lesson coming up. Fletch figured if he could get to understand it beforehand, he'd speak up next day in class and shine a little for Miss Dokstra.

It was a whole set of problems about some Mr. Walsh who bought a life insurance policy. The idea was to find out whether Mr. Walsh would make more money out of insurance or if he saved his money in a bank, depending on how long he lived. It was decimals mostly, easy enough. Fletch proved pretty good at simple arithmetic even though the fingers of his left hand, flat on the table as he wrote, did move a little to help him add and subtract. By the time we finished, he seemed to have caught on to the idea of the problem pretty good.

"You're okay, Henry Three," Fletch slammed his pencil into the book. "You make it clear as a bell."

"It's not me." I gathered the papers we'd worked over. "You manage real fine, once you get the hang of it. What makes you think you need so much help?"

"Well, it's only there's questions that come up." Fletch shrugged. "And who wants to keep asking Dokstra to stop, all the time, to keep explaining things just for me? With all the rest of them sitting there, thinking the way they do."

"About poison?"

"Not that I care what they think. It's just that I'd like to show them once in a while that I'm up with all the rest and maybe even out front a little." He stacked his books. "Like tomorrow, just watch me. Once I take a swing at Mr. Walsh, I'm going all the way. Right around the bases."

I watched him. But it didn't turn out so well that next day

38

in class. Miss Dokstra was surprised enough, coming to the new lesson, when Fletch volunteered to show the rest of us how to work out insurance. And up at the blackboard he laid the problem out just right. But it was the compound interest that floored Fletch. He forgot you had to figure interest on each year's saving separately. Once he made that slip, everything else went wrong.

Up in front of the class, Fletch slowed down and started whispering to himself. Miss Dokstra made a suggestion but he stopped her. "I don't need coaching," he said. "I got this stuff cold." But pretty soon he was erasing more than he was writing. Even the arithmetic went sour, with three times four ending up fourteen. Fletch was in a sweat. You heard giggles.

"You've given it a good try, Fletcher." Miss Dokstra took the chalk away from him. "But perhaps I'd better take over," she turned, "unless there's someone else who thinks he can work it out for us?"

Instead of heading for his seat, Fletch just stood and looked at me. He waited for me to answer. As if I were involved! Except of course, I knew how to work the thing out.

"You can go to your seat, Fletcher," Miss Dokstra reminded him.

"But there is someone else!" Fletch was hoarse, mad as he was at himself. "He can show you."

"Who?" Miss Dokstra looked around the class.

Everyone stared where Fletch stared, in a beeline straight at me. I tried smiling around, here and there, and took care of the itch that came across the back of my neck. I didn't see why Larkin was dragging me into it. I wasn't going to move, waiting for Fletch to sing out my name, no matter what happened. No one spoke. They all stared.

Until Dokstra put an end to it. "That'll be all, Fletcher," she said. "It looks as if we could all use some help in buying insurance."

There was nothing funny to the remark. But someone laughed. And then the whole place went, roaring at Fletch as he walked back to his seat. I couldn't help but join in, not to laugh at Larkin, but with the relief I felt the thing was all over. Besides, everyone was on my side. A couple of them even mentioned the nerve Larkin had for trying to put me, the newest kid in class, on a spot. Dokstra banged a book a couple of times for quiet. And that was the end of Fletcher Larkin going all the way around the bases.

But I didn't see what right he had to get so disgusted at me. I felt his look from the rear boring into the back of my head. I turned. Fletcher sat there staring at me the way you'd study what was getting soft around the edges and starting to rot. He followed me into the BOYS right before lunch where there was no one else.

"It's all off," he pointed. "The whole deal's off."

"Why?"

'How could you sit there without even standing up for yourself?"

"Where does that come into it?"

"It's just that I'm not making any deal with a guy who won't even show who he is."

"But you weren't supposed to notice me. That was the trade."

"It's finished. Any trade. You're turning out no different from any of the others."

"What does that mean? That you're going to tell them?"

"I ought to." Fletcher's finger banged me on the chest. "And I am! That's just what I'm going to do."

4

ALL THROUGH THAT FIRST WEEK AND UP UNTIL THE END
of my birthday party on Friday afternoon, Crestview for me
was worse than walking across the ice of a late winter pond.
I kept waiting for a crack to come along, one fast crack out
of Fletcher Larkin, and then the whole place would break
up with nowhere for me to go but down.

I tried to catch his eye in school, I waited behind a
hedge along the way he went home, I even showed up at The
Mansion one night where Louie Gamero said he was too
busy to come to the door. He wouldn't talk to me.

There was nothing fair about it. I was ready to go through
with my part of the deal. Except me standing up in class,
making a show of myself, that wasn't part of what we agreed
about. Where would it do him any good, was all I wanted
to know, if it ended up the same for me in Crestview as

everywhere else? He had to give me some kind of chance.

All that week there was no way to tell about anything that happened, when it was going to collapse. Plenty happened. Even in class that first morning I got handed a paper before the noon time bell, with seven names on it. That's the way they chose sides for the stick ball game the gang of them played after lunch and, I gathered, they wanted me to sign up for one of the teams. I put my name down. I played. I even got a hit, a scratch single. Every day they asked me to play.

The big thing that first week in Crestview, though, was my own party. It was Ma's idea to turn the birthday I had into a real affair. It was on account of our furniture. I didn't get the connection myself until Ma explained. It seemed our ranch type furniture was way out of style for New York City. Ma didn't see how we could invite any neighbors in to visit until we bought a whole new houseful of furniture.

That was going to cost. And depending on how fast Dad firmed things up at the office, it might be months before we were redecorated. In between, Ma and Dad couldn't go accepting invitations from people, seeing there was no way to pay them back. Socially, Ma pointed out, it put us in a hole.

So the inspiration Ma had was to pay everyone back beforehand. To leave most of our furniture packed and invite the neighbors to a cocktail party in the backyard. Soon enough that is, so we still had the excuse there wasn't time to fix the house up. It was a neat enough way to handle the situation if we could find a reason to throw a party so quick, before we hardly knew anybody. So my birthday, just a couple of days away, was perfect.

"If you don't mind?" my mother asked me.

"What?"

"Getting used for a reason. Along with the boys in your class we'd have the opportunity to invite their parents as well."

"Why should I mind you giving me a birthday party?"

"Because we're using you. It's in a good cause, Henry. But this is the only time you'll ever turn thirteen. So you're the one to pass on it."

"It's fine with me," I told my mother. "I mean as far as I'm concerned, it's great."

The way I put it was no more than keeping my fingers crossed. The one most concerned was Fletcher Larkin. Along with everything else, he could wreck my birthday party too. They weren't getting invited, of course, the Larkins, considering how everyone felt about them. And I didn't know how Fletch would take that, little chance as he gave me to talk to him. But all through the week and most of Friday, Fletch never made a move.

So nothing stopped my Ma from going to work at least. She sent telegrams signed by me to invite everybody. Then she searched around for a celebrity to be my guest of honor. The one Ma found was a girl she used to know named Annie Ryan who turned out to be Sandra Shaw, the nurse you see every Thursday on *Young Doctor Muldane* over Channel Four. Ma talked her into coming.

The importance of a celebrity, as I understand it, was to have someone around people were interested to meet even if they weren't so interested to met us Loverings. Not only did it guarantee a large turnout, but also a celebrity made

44

sure the big ones would come. Like Mr. Driscoll who was very big at Manufacturer's Trust Company and Mr. Sattersly who was very big at Time, Inc. It worked the way Ma planned. Once the news got around Sandra Shaw was showing up in Crestview both of those called and a lot of others as well, to say how delighted they were.

Besides, Ma invited three other girls she knew in New York. With everyone in Crestview so close, Ma thought it would be a novelty to have some faces around that didn't look too familiar. Especially, if they were pretty. That'd give any husbands who felt like it a chance to have someone to flirt with. As novelties for the wives, Dad was bringing a couple of Junior Executives from the office, Jack Lemmon types.

For entertainment, Ma hired a man named Luis de Alberich who played a guitar. Only we were going to let on he was a friend we knew from New Mexico, so no one would think we were trying to put on a professional show. Agnes was bringing in two extra maids from Harlem. One was to feed those my age at a special table over near the garage. It was going to be a barbecue supper; hamburgers and hot dogs and cole slaw and baked beans and roasted corn and French Fries along with four different kinds of ice cream to eat with my birthday cake.

There wasn't any food for the grownups except stuff Ma made that you could eat with your left hand. The right hand has to be left free, at a cocktail party, for drinking. Agnes, who had a lot of experience serving drinks, checked with the other maids around town to make sure she bought everyone's favorite liquor.

I never saw a party better organized, the way Ma handled

it. Friday morning, Sis stayed home from school to decorate the backyard with Agnes and the two extra ladies. By the time I showed up after class, I couldn't recognize the place. The backyard was a room practically, with paper streamers in red, yellow and purple curling from the four sides of the garden up to a point so it seemed you were standing under a curved roof. Hanging down below, here and there, were Chinese lanterns.

I began to think maybe everything would turn out all right. At least, it didn't seem Fletcher Larkin had in mind to ruin my birthday. Besides the comments I heard from the others in class were pretty hopeful. Mine was the first birthday party since school started and everyone expected to have a real good time.

And they certainly did. The whole thing went off like clockwork. Sandra Shaw and the pretty girls and the Jack Lemmon types, even though they didn't look like any Jack Lemmon I ever saw, all of them made a fine impression. Mr. Luis de Alberich, after we begged him to play, turned out to be first class on the guitar. We expected he'd play all Spanish but the first thing came out was "Happy Birthday." I had to stand there while everyone joined in but I managed all right, considering I never had a party before, when it came to blowing out the candles and slicing the cake.

Our food was a success. Ma's specialties for the grown-ups caused a lot of conversation. Her *Guacamole Salad* on toasted *tortillas* was a Mexican dish that opened up a chance to tell about Sante Fe and how Dad had been a consultant for the missile program at Los Alamos. And the *Chicken Liver Strudel* she made brought up the Pennsylvania Dutch and how Dad used to be the managing director of General Magneto, a plant A. L. & L. had near Easton. By the time much got eaten, most everyone had heard a good deal about the Loverings, which was the main idea for having the party to begin with.

I collected a lot of presents, mostly kits to build things out of plastic. But Dad gave me a battery operated electric record player which I never expected. And from Ma I got a skin diver's outfit, the rubber suit and mask and fins and spear gun, which couldn't be neater seeing that it's my best sport, swimming. Besides, for those my age, there were a lot of games set up in the garage plus a movie projector that showed a full hour of cartoons.

It was certainly the best birthday party a thirteen-year-old could have. The roar that came out of our backyard, all the talk and laughing, had to be heard a block away. And with the parked cars stretching both sides down the street, you could see that the impact of the Loverings was pretty solid. The backyard couldn't hold more people. "Almost a hundred percent turnout," Ma whispered. And it looked as if the whole crowd were really glad we'd showed up to make our home in Crestview. I never imagined we'd be so lucky.

Except a red streamer fluttered to the ground.

It was cut neat as with a scissor. A low whirr spit into the bushes behind me. And another streamer, yellow, started to uncurl. A Chinese lantern jumped and rocked and broke into flame. That was the end of our luck, I figured.

I ran for the lantern. So did my father. One of the Jack Lemmons helped too. We pulled the fire down before it spread and stamped out the blaze on the grass.

A freak breeze, that's what my father thought. I knew

different. So did Chuck Driscoll who was right behind me and Ray Sattersley. They heard it too, the scratch through the streamers, the flick at the wall of the garage.

"It's a BB gun," thought Ray.

"Or a slingshot," Chuck looked around.

"Larkin," I said.

"It'd be like him," Ray agreed.

Another streamer split, waved into the air and settled down on the crowd. "What a lovely effect," said Mrs. Lathrop. "Like a paper fountain. Is that going to happen to all of them?"

"No ma'm, I hope not," I pushed past her. I found a chair and climbed with my head through the streamers. Trees, roofs and television aerials were all I saw. No Larkin.

"The direction it's coming from," Chuck Driscoll pulled me down, "he has to be over toward Magnolia Avenue."

Ray elbowed ahead of us. "We can spot him from the Simpsons."

The two of us took after Ray through the hedge into the garden next door. The Simpsons had a pool with a slide for their two small girls. I made it up the ladder of the slide. Then I saw him. He sat on the roof of a garage over toward Magnolia Avenue. Chuck Driscoll was right. He had a slingshot.

"Larkin!" That was as much as I could get out of me. It went dry inside and closed up and hard.

I fell off the slide and started running. There was a whimper, a dog's noise, and it came from me as I ran. I fought my way through rose bushes, past the tearing branches and over a fence. I ran. I wanted to leave Crestview behind. After all the waiting for what Larkin would do, there was nothing left. There was no way to stop him from breaking up my birthday party. No way to keep him from telling all about me. But even so, with nothing to do, I rounded the garage and came to where he was. He sat comfortable up top, one foot swinging from the roof of the garage as he lifted a dried bean into his slingshot. He stopped to watch me catch my breath.

"Please," I managed to ask him. "Go away."

"Well, I didn't plan on coming." He gave me that big smile of his. "But thinking it over, Henry Three, no one knows you better than I do." He let go with a shot. "So I thought I'd show up and make the party complete."

"You could hurt somebody with that thing," Chuck Driscoll came up behind me. "Lay off or we'll brain you."

"No one's going to get hurt," Fletch laughed at him. "Unless you guys try something."

"Who has to mess with Larkin?" asked Ray Sattersley. "One quick call and a squad car shows up. They'll take care of him."

"Sure, go ahead and call the cops." Fletch went to looking for another bean. "Then it'll be in all the papers, too."

"What'll be in all the papers?" asked Chuck.

"Some of the things I have to tell them. They could even put it out over T.V."

"Who cares what you tell them?" Ray started away from the garage.

"Maybe Henry Three, he does." Fletch loaded the slingshot.

Ray turned. "Do you?"

There was only a small boulder to look at, stuck in the flower bed next to the garage. I studied the boulder, the

49

crack that ran through it and the rounded top. "It's just that you'd better not," I explained to Ray. "Not make any calls, that is."

"But you can't let him get away with busting up your birthday." Ray stared at me.

"You got to do something," said Chuck.

Fletcher Larkin was a trap I couldn't get out of. What's worse, he turned blurred and took on a watery look.

"Do something? Not Henry Three." Fletcher stretched the sling and let it go again. "Henry's not out to do anything around here."

"No?" It was a high squeak that forced my throat open again. Without even thinking, I was headed for the rock. I had a running start. I picked up speed enough to come off the top of the rock like it was a springboard. It gave me the height to reach for Fletcher's sneaker. I had his ankle.

Fletch yelled. But I had too much leverage for him. He slipped and came loose, falling all the way and landing on top of me.

I tried to grab a leg that got away and then I had a wrist, his right hand. He yanked to free it and he pulled me to my feet. I slipped. But I still had the wrist.

I had him.

I had his right hand twisted against his back. It was the hold I knew about a, kind of half nelson. I lifted, reaching to shove that right hand of his across his back, hard up against his left shoulder.

"Look out!" He screamed, Fletch did, doubling over and ducking to get free and I kicked at his right leg until it buckled and he went down. I had his wrist to pull now like a rope, instead of to push, and I hauled at it harder with every breath I took.

"Okay," I whispered to Fletch. "Go ahead and tell them. Go ahead!"

Then it scared me, what could happen to the arm I was pulling at. "Go ahead," I begged. "If you want to tell them, go ahead."

"No, Hank," I heard Chuck Driscoll. "Look out for his shoulder."

"What're you doing?" Fletch screamed. "Let me go."

"Not until you promise."

He rolled his face in the grass and his body went loose. "Leave me be!"

"Then promise me you'll never tell them." I spoke into his ear, no louder than a breath. "Just promise. That's all."

It came like a cough. "Okay," was what I heard.

"Okay, what?"

"I won't tell. I promise. Let me be!"

I got up. The three of us stood there, Chuck Driscoll, Ray Sattersley and I. Face down in the grass, Fletcher Larkin didn't move. Even his right hand stayed where I left it, tight against his back. Then the hand crawled slow across the T-shirt, feeling its way like a crab on a rock, until it edged out of sight beneath his body.

He lay still. There was a twitch to his shoulders. But when he turned to stare up into the night that was coming, the look he had was clear enough. He seemed all right.

He sat up and came to his feet. He walked over to the flower bed and looked around. It was the slingshot he was trying to find. When he did, he wrapped it up neat and put it into his back pocket. He walked down to the end of the garage and he stopped there, leaning against the corner

51

with his back to us.

I managed a deep breath and the smell of Crestview was the flowers in the early evening and the fresh cut grass.

Fletch turned and, instead of any hurt on his face, it was a surprise to see there was even the beginning of a smile in the way he looked at me. "I guess I can't beef this time, Henry Three, how you stood up for yourself." He rubbed his shoulder and he held it. "So maybe you got it coming to you. Why not?" he asked himself. "Happy Birthday," he said and then he left us.

5

It was bigger than any present, even the battery operated record player and the skin diver's suit, what I got from Fletch for my birthday. I got rid of him. I was safe. Fletcher Larkin was shut up for good and I had the chance now, if I could handle it, to live same as any other kid in Crestview. It was a miracle it happened so quickly, how in three or four minutes there was no more problem.

To everyone else the miracle was me, personally. It was the first time in Crestview a fight with Larkin ever ended the way it had with me. And the news, when we got back to the party, caused a stir. Ray did all the talking and Chuck Driscoll put on a repeat of the battle that looked like a cross between *Wagons West* and Gorgeous George, the wrestler. It turned me into as much of an attraction, almost, as Sandra Shaw. And when I told the truth to all the questions that came along, I mean how lucky I was, that made it even better. Everyone had the idea I was modest.

"Don't you play it cool with me." Ma came to her knees beside me. "Into the kitchen," she whispered, "where I can look you over."

"I'm all right," I convinced her.

Dad couldn't have been more satisfied, the way I showed my physical courage with Larkin. "Crestview's secret weapon," was what he called me. "When the Pentagon hears about this I bet we get the contract to turn you out in quantity."

And that's the way it went for the rest of the party, remarks on that order. I ended up practically a celebrity, you might say, on my own. Next morning after breakfast there was a bunch of kids peeking through the bushes from the Simpsons next door, third and fourth graders. I thought they were watching Agnes and her friends take down the decorations. But when I came out to head off some dog rampaging around the place, rolling himself into red and yellow streamers, the gang of them yelled, "That's him!"

The dog stopped and came zigzagging up to me, a combination wirehaired terrier, poodle and helicopter, from the action his ears had. The bark came out of him sounded like laughing. "Who belongs to this hound?" I shouted.

It was a red-headed seven-year-old who crawled through the hedge. "You're him," he pointed. "I bet you. You're Number Three."

"Henry Three," I told him.

He turned to his gang back in ambush. "He's him, all right. The one who licked Fletcher Larkin." The way the boy and the dog examined me, I could've been something in

a store window. "Any chance," the redhead asked, "of seeing your fist?"

I showed him my closed right hand. He felt it. "Wow," he decided, "Full of muscles."

The hedge over at the Simpsons filled with faces. "I dare you go ahead and ask him, Shep," one of them yelled.

The redhead turned out to be Shep Untermeyer, the kid brother of a fellow in my class. The dog's name was Winner. "I don't suppose you'd even think," asked Shep, "about an autograph? About giving me one."

"Sure. Where's your pencil and paper?"

"That's the trouble. I don't have any.

We settled on a strip of yellow streamer. I tore three holes in it. "This gives you the last of my name anyway."

"Three," Shep counted.

"The most important part," I told him.

"And the color couldn't be better." Shep agreed. He climbed back through the bushes with Winner and the crowd of them gathered around to inspect my autograph.

There was a phone call just then, for me. That's what really told us how well we were making out in Crestview, the telephone. It started ringing that Saturday morning and pretty soon, whenever you saw Sis, she was out of breath. Within four days she wore a new pair of pink house slippers to a frazzle, sliding in to grab the receiver.

In no time at all, Ma and Dad were booked solid for the next couple of weeks with everyone trying to pay us back for the good time they had at my party. So many invitations came in for dinner and bridge and cocktails, Dad hardly had any time for the work he brought home every night. But visiting around in Crestview was just as important in

56

giving Dad the boost he needed at the office. Some of our neighbors, like Mr. Driscoll and Mr. Sattersley, had a lot of influence at A. L. & L. So getting in with people like that could only improve Dad's chances.

Pretty quick too, Sis had a fine collection of fellows started; a couple of tall ones, and a blond one with big ears who played tennis, and Warren Andrews with heavy glasses. The argument started up again between Sis and Ma, about when she got in the night before, and that made it seem like we were really settling down to make our home in Crestview.

Even Lady that first weekend was invited to a picnic with the Simpson kids next door.

But me, I was the big surprise. For the first time in my life I actually had to write down the different invitations I had and what time people were expecting me. On that Saturday and Sunday alone, after my birthday, I had six invitations.

First, I went sailing in a cabin cruiser with Al Sommers and his folks out of a yacht club there was in Crest Cove. Two, I played right field for the Crestview Little League against Larkshaven and I managed to get a two base hit, even though we lost. Three and four, I went swimming in two different pools, the Sattersleys' and the Driscolls', which was fine with me considering I do all right in the swimming department. Five, Mike Buell let me work his father's short wave transmitter, 2LBW, and I talked to someone in Adelaide, Australia. And six, I stayed overnight with Arnie Untermeyer and we looked at color television along with his kid brother Shep and Winner, the peculiar looking dog who was forever laughing.

It was hard to get used to, all the attention that came my

way. I thought it was only because I was the first one lucky enough to beat Larkin in a fight. But even after that wore off, people were still interested to see me. I mean when I walked into Pirelli's Pharmacy, any booth I wanted to sit in, the crowd would shove over to make room for me. I could talk about anything and I'd get along fine. There were kids who kept going out of their way to get in touch with me, like calling or coming by the house. They were starting to be friends of mine, was the way it appeared.

And the best part was, I didn't have to worry. There was no chance anyone would find out about me, as long as it depended on Fletcher Larkin. I was pretty sure you could trust Fletch, hard as it was to get that promise out of him. And I was right. Fletch couldn't care less what went on with the rest of us. The couple of times I nodded when we happened to meet, as if to thank him, all I got out of him was a laugh.

Fine as everything was working out, the only problem left really was Miss Dokstra. She seemed to go out of her way to ask me questions whenever anything came up that she wanted to discuss in class. There was no doubt what a fine teacher she was compared to most I've had. But I never let myself go too far, day after day.

"Is anything wrong?" Miss Dokstra stopped me one afternoon. "I've been wondering, Henry, whether you're happy here in Crestview."

"I certainly am."

"But we don't seem to be inspiring you to any great lengths, as far as achievement goes. I couldn't help wondering whether it was our fault."

"I don't see where it's anyone's fault. I thought I was

doing all right."

"You are." Miss Dokstra went to work on her hair with the pencil she had. "Just a shade better than average."

"That's good enough, isn't it?"

"Not for you," she said. "Considering your potential. There's always the hope, you know, of finding a scholar to work with someday. If there's any way I can help, I'll be glad to."

"Thanks, Miss Dokstra," I told her.

But I didn't see where I needed any help. I'd never got along so good on my own. Maybe the class work wasn't so interesting this way. But the papers that came around every morning made up for that, the ones they used to choose up teams for stickball. Sometimes the sheets for the two sides showed up at my desk in a dead heat. And it had nothing to do with the kind of a ballplayer I am. Both sides wanted to show how friendly they were, that's all.

I had a whole crowd now that I ran with. It was as much a kick as I'd always expected it would be. I mean, just to yell at a guy across his backyard and find he was glad I'd come around. Or to pedal up to a gang of them and see the bikes open up so I could pull in with the rest. And then it got to be even better than that. From belonging to a crowd, the chance came along to become a member of the most important group there was in Crestview, the X15.

There were only three who belonged to it, Gardner Klein and Ray Sattersley in my class and Pete Feddersen who was in the grade ahead of ours. They were the biggest wheels in school and their reputation depended mostly on the X15. It was an automobile. They owned it. Those three had to be the only ones our age on Long Island, or in the entire United

States for that matter, who actually owned their own automobile.

The thing is, it was an automobile that they built. Their Dads acted as consultants. And Marty Steinhoff of *Steinhoff's Twenty-Four Hour Gas* out on the Turnpike lent them a lot of tools. But mostly it was Ray and Pete and Gardner who did the work. With the year and a half advance they got on their allowance, the three of them scoured the junkyards around for all the parts and, finally, there were pieces of fifteen different automobiles that went into their car. Which is how it got the name, X15.

It was kept in back of Feddersen's garage, the car was, under a cover. Very few ever saw it, private as Ray and Pete and Gardner kept their automobile. And it was rare, a real special occasion, when any kid got invited to ride in it. When someone did, he showed up at school the next morning marveling about the X15 but never explaining, along with Ray and Pete and Gardner, where they went riding to or how any of them were able to drive the car at all. There were years we had to wait before any of us could get a licence.

I was invited. Along with all the other attention that came my way, the three of them took me over to Feddersen's backyard one afternoon. It was an honor, just getting asked. But I couldn't see how they were even going to move the car out from behind Feddersen's garage, wedged in as it was by the hedges and bushes growing all around.

Once the nylon tarp came off though, you couldn't help but wonder at the X15. It was the smoothest black four-door sedan, with all its chrome sparkling, you'd ever want to see. She didn't look like any particular kind of car, Ford, Chevie, or whatever, and her lines were more up and down than any recent model. But the shape she was in, you'd think the X15 was standing in a showroom. "How'd you ever do it?" I asked.

"Muscle," said Feddersen.

"Paint, paint, paint," said Klein. "And polish, polish, polish."

"Get in," said Ray.

It even smelled new.

"Marty Steinhoff gave us the smell." Feddersen took the wheel. "Came in a spritz can." He released the brake, started the motor and shifted into first while the car never moved. The three of them turned to me in the back seat and waited to hear what I had to say. I didn't know what to say.

"Listen to that motor," Ray suggested.

I listened. "It sounds fine," I had to agree. "But I was wondering, doesn't anything else get to happen?"

"Sure," said Ray. "Just keep listening." He shifted and we listened to the motor in second and, after he shifted again, we listened to the motor in high. The three kept turning around to hear my comments. "It sounds just fine," was the best I could do. "But the fact is," I couldn't help mentioning, "you don't go anywhere. Not that you have to," I told them, "when you've got such a fine motor to listen to."

"How can we go anywhere," asked Ray, "without any of us has a licence?"

"The car's jacked up on blocks," explained Gardner, "The wheels are off the ground, so how can it go?"

"Besides," Pete looked around from the wheel, "where do you want to go?"

"Nowhere," I said. "Nowhere in particular."

"Then you wouldn't want better than the X15," said Pete. "It's about the greatest car in the world for going nowhere." He switched on the radio and it came through loud and clear, four electric guitars. "Just sit back and enjoy yourself."

I leaned back into the vinyl seat covers. "Maybe you're right. As long as you're going no place, what could be better than this?"

"Now you're getting the idea," said Ray. "The X15 gives you all the pleasures of driving with none of the headaches. No speed cops. No traffic. No getting caught in line bumper to bumper. And parking's a cinch. We don't have to cruise around for half an hour to find someplace to pull into."

"Besides the scenery," I pointed out, "couldn't be cleaner. No billboards. No roadstands."

"Who says no roadstands?" Pete stopped the car. "What'll you guys have, drinks, cones, candy bars? You name it."

We all wanted something to drink. Pete was out of the car, across the garden and back from his kitchen in just about a minute. "Where's the stand," he passed around the bottles, "would give you any better service than this?"

They were certainly happy with themselves. Ray and Pete and Gardner. And no one had a better right, far as I could see. It had to be wonderful to be a part of anything like the X15. "Besides which," Ray described, "it's long term. There's no wear to the X15, not even to the rubber. She just sits here getting the best of treatment waiting for us to grow up. Once we do, soon as we get our licence, no one has to ask the family can we use the car tonight. We're in business with our own transportation."

"Meanwhile," Pete started up again, "just listen to that motor."

We'd driven about four miles according to the speedometer, so Pete hauled the wheel around and drove back four miles to get us where we started from. The way he did it began an idea circulating that I couldn't help thinking about. The others kept listening to the motor, which they talked about in a language that was way beyond me, like *cylinder bore* and *axle ratio* and *rpm* and *oversteer*. They could've been a secret society using code as far as I was concerned, or maybe they went on that way just to impress me.

They didn't have to go to all that trouble. I was only hoping the three of them would ask me again, sometime. When all of a sudden the idea that was circulating started to develop into sort of a plan for operating the X15 that looked real interesting. I was just on the point of telling them about it, so that maybe I'd be sure to get a second invitation. When another thought occured.

Why shouldn't I try to become a member of the X15? It took a lot of nerve just to ask the question. The fact is I was doing fine enough in Crestview. I had plenty of reason to be satisfied. But there's no more fun, far as I'm concerned, than to get hold of an idea and think it out to see if it'll actually work. So I took a chance.

When we were stretching the nylon cover back on the car, I said, "I'm sorry I don't belong to the X15."

"Most kids are," admitted Gardner.

"Not only on my account," I mentioned. "I know it's fine listening to the engine, but the X15's got a lot of potential that ought to be worked out."

"For instance?" asked Ray.

"Well, there's Niagara Falls," I suggested. "You could take a trip up there. Or Yellowstone Park. Or the Grand Canyon. You could even go around the world."

"What're you talking about?" yelled Gardner. "The X15 doesn't move!"

"Well, you take any car, there's always something a little wrong with it. All it means is, you have to think up a different way to handle the problem."

"Where would thinking get you with the X15?" Ray wanted to know.

"Around the world maybe."

"How?"

"That's why I'm sorry I don't belong," I pulled my corner of the cover tight. "Where do I come off telling you fellows how to run the X15? That's up to the members isn't it? I'm thankful enough you invited me along for the ride. I wouldn't want to butt in with suggestions how to handle your own automobile."

"But suppose we asked you?" said Pete.

"To make a suggestion?"

"What I mean," Pete turned to the others. "Suppose he did show us some way to go around the world?"

"It'd be magic," said Gardner.

"But if he's got some kind of an idea, and we liked it, there's nothing against us having another member, is there?"

"I think we ought to have a meeting," said Ray.

The three of them closed in together on the other side of the car and I waited. There was a good deal of arguing went on, mostly with Gardner saying, "It's impossible," but when they headed back Pete nodded. "You take us around the world, Henry Three, and you're a member of the X15."

"Okay."

"Tomorrow afternoon?" asked Gardner.

"Why not?"

6

IT WAS A SIMPLE ENOUGH IDEA. THE X15 DIDN'T MOVE.
But the speedometer did. You could actually cover all the
miles you wanted in the X15, according to the speedometer.
If you wanted to reach some place that was five miles away
it was easy enough to tell, by the speedometer at least,
when you got there. That was simple enough.

And along with that, you take a map. It's mostly miles.
The big thing about a map, it gives you the miles to the next
town coming up or the next turn you have to make. It was
easy to see that the X15 could travel across a map even if it
couldn't travel down a road.

So as long as you made the right turns and clocked the
right mileage, there wasn't any place on a map you couldn't
get to. Whether it was five miles or fifty or five thousand
miles away. Everywhere in the world is on a map. As long

as that was the case, the X15 could get there.

On a map that is. And out of all the auto maps we had at home, I put together a set that would take us clear across the United States. Plus, I made a collection of highway guides and pamphlets. So we could read about the different places we hit, its scenery and history and manufacturing and the best motels and restaurants. That night I put in as much time at the dining room table polishing up my idea as Dad, who was working on his reorganization plan for A. L. & L.

The next afternoon, I brought all my stuff over to the X15 in a zip bag. I got in behind the wheel to do the driving. Then I tried to explain the whole thing to Ray and Pete and Gardner. None of them said whether they liked the idea. I don't know how much of what I told them actually got through.

"For instance," Ray nodded when I finished. "Let's see how it works."

"There's just one more thing." I pointed out the mileage total on the speedometer. "That last number on the end, the red one."

"That marks a tenth of a mile?" asked Gardner.

"That one. All you've got to remember is that from now on that red number counts for a mile. Every red number coming up stands for one whole mile. All right with you?"

"Sure," said Pete. "That's the easiest part."

"Okay then." I was a little nervous starting the motor. "First place we head for is New York City." Shifting into first I made a right turn to get out of the Feddersen driveway. I made a left turn down Havenhurst Drive to get to Moriches Boulevard.

"From here," I checked with them, "we make another left turn and it's one mile to the North Shore Turnpike."

"Correct," said Ray.

I made the turn and all of us watched the next red number come up on the speedometer.

"This is it," said Ray. "The North Shore Turnpike."

Pete did the navigating. Spread out on his lap was the map NEW YORK CITY AND VICINITY. We had to turn right and head for the Mid-Island Expressway that would take us straight to New York. To find the mileage I gave Pete a beaded chain that came off a key ring. He laid the chain along the road between us and the Expressway and measured the length against the mileage scale down in the corner of the map.

"You make a right turn and it's seventeen miles to the Expressway," Pete told me.

"Take off," said Ray. "You know, this idea, maybe it's got possibilities. Let's get into New York City."

I stepped on the gas but after about three miles Pete, with his eyes fixed on the speedometer, yelled, "No, you don't."

"Don't what?" I asked.

"Go fifty miles an hour."

"Why not?"

"At this time of day?" Pete pointed at his watch. "Ten after five? This stretch is murder. The Trans-American airplane factory lets out. And there's Arco Transistor and two other plants. They all quit at five. You get caught here at this hour and you're frozen stiff. Eight, ten miles an hour is the best you'd ever do."

I slowed to eight.

"Aw come on," it was the first time Gardner spoke up. "Now we're on our way, I'd just as soon get into New York."

"In this traffic?" said Ray. "Pete's right. We're lucky to be crawling."

"Where's traffic," Gardner turned Pete around. "You told Henry yourself, the X15 don't get caught in traffic."

"That's going nowhere," said Pete. "When you're going

69

somewhere down an actual road on a real map, you have to ride the road the way it is, don't you?"

"Only stands to reason," said Ray.

"Well, if that's the way you're going to work it," Gardner bent past me and leaned on the horn. "Maybe that'll loosen the line, up ahead."

"You know," smiled Pete. "I think it did spread them some. Go ahead, Hank, squeeze it a bit."

I let the X15 ride up to fifteen miles an hour. It looked as if the three of them were taking hold of the idea. As long as they were bringing up their own different angles, they had to think the notion was at least good. So the more back seat driving went on, the better.

At the Mid-Island Expressway we went into a clover leaf and straightened out for New York City twenty-four miles ahead. The three of them agreed that the traffic was all the other way now, everyone coming home from the city, and that we had three empty lanes practically to ourselves. I stepped on it and at fifty five miles an hour, the little red numbers flew up in a steady stream. We made the twenty four miles in a little over two minutes.

"How do you like that?" Ray banged the seat behind my ear. "After we put in all that time getting the X15 to run like any other car, with one idea Henry Three gives us jet propulsion. We really go!"

It was a comfort to hear how the others chimed in. I was almost starting to enjoy the trip myself as we slowed down for the toll booth at the tunnel that took us into New York. Pete handed me a quarter to pay the toll. I passed it out the window and gave it back to him. That was okay with everyone but most of the time the X15 was filled with arguments;

70

about the best streets to get cross town in New York, about the home-going traffic we hit through the tunnel under the Hudson River, and about the thunder shower that came at us as we pulled on to our next map, NEW JERSEY.

Even though the sun was shining in Crestview, the radio announced it was pouring buckets on Highway 80, where we were traveling. Pete won the discussion and we rolled up our windows to keep the rain out, plus, I switched on the wipers. That's the way we drove for the next ten, twelve minutes eating up the seventy miles across New Jersey. Once we crossed the Delaware River and headed into our third map, PENNSYLVANIA, the weather cleared and we were able to get some fresh air back into the X15.

We used the Pennsylvania Turnpike from then on. It costs you two cents a mile but it's certainly worth it. The Turnpike connects up with Thruways that take you all the way out to Chicago without an intersection or a red light. You wouldn't want better for making time.

By now you got the feeling we were really heading west, the way the mountains built up. These were different parts of the Appalachians according to the pamphlet Ray read to us. It sounded pretty rugged, especially as you got out toward Pittsburgh where the steel mills are. But driving the Turnpike was simple enough, without any curves hardly to look out for. What we hit a lot of was long tunnels, cut right through the biggest mountains, where I had to remember to put on my headlights.

By the time we drove on to our next map, OHIO, we were all pretty busy in the X15. Along with me driving and Pete navigating and Ray reading about the places going by, a big debate started over the route we ought to take out to the west coast. The three of them seemed to take it for granted that we were on our way, that we were going right around the world.

I thought by this time someone ought to mention me, whether the idea was good enough to make me a member of the X15. I didn't want to bring up any suggestion like that myself. Besides you couldn't get a word into all the yelling that went on, whether we ought to keep north through Nevada or head south for Arizona.

It was Gardner broke it up. We were streaming past Cleveland when he looked at his watch. "Hey, pull out of here," Gardner yelled. "Today's my piano lesson. I got to get home."

I turned off at the next Thruway exit, a place called Shaker Heights, and killed the motor when Ray asked Gardner, "How?"

"How what?" said Gardner.

"How're you going to get home?"

"How do I always get home? I hop Pete's fence, go through Talmadge's backyard and walk across the street."

"Not from here, you don't. You don't walk home. You're in Cleveland, Ohio."

"Say that's right." Gardner looked at me. "We're in Cleveland."

"We can't drive back." Ray rested his chin on the back of the driver's seat, "or we lose all the mileage we piled up. How'll we ever get around the world if we have to come back to Crestview every day."

"You know," said Gardner. "I thought this was too good to be true. How about it?" he asked me. "How do I get to my piano lesson from Cleveland, Ohio?"

72

"It's nothing to worry about," I tried to tell them. Though personally, I was worried enough about this part myself. I did have it all thought out from the night before but there was no way to be sure whether it was going to work or not. "First of all, we have to get out of the car."

The three of them came around to my side as I slammed the door behind me. "The thing is, you fellows don't want to lose sight of the facts. And the plain fact is that right this second you're in Crestview, aren't you?"

Pete shook his head. "That's hard to say."

"But look around you."

"Well, if that's all you want to go by," said Gardner. "Then sure, we're in Crestview."

"Now you're looking at the facts," I tried to explain.

"Oh no you don't," said Pete. "We're not going to buy that, Henry Three. How can we be in Cleveland, Ohio, and back here in Crestview at one and the same time?" He shook his head. "That's infantile."

"No, Pete, I wouldn't say that. Actually, if you want to come right down to it, it's scientific."

"Like how?"

"You heard of relativity?"

"Who hasn't?" asked Pete. "Where does that come into it?"

"Well, in relativity the place you're in or the speed you're going all depends on the way you look at it." The three of them watched my hands as I tried to show what I meant. "You're standing at a railroad track and a train comes by at sixty miles an hour. Then that's the speed it's going at, isn't it?"

"Check," said Ray.

"Relative to you, that is."

"Double check," said Ray.

"But if you're driving in a car doing sixty alongside that track then, relative to you, the trains not moving at all."

"How's that again?" asked Pete.

"No, he's right." Ray moved his hands the same as I did. "If you're doing sixty and you look at the train it just stays there in the same place all the time. It doesn't move."

"That's the idea," I told Ray. "It's only when the driver in the car notices something else, like the telegraph poles going by or his speedometer, that he sees he's moving fast."

"That's clear enough."

"It's relative."

"I'm with you," said Ray.

"It's the same here. If you go back into the X15 and you check the speedometer, you can see we've done better than six hundred miles this afternoon. Relative to the speedometer we're in Cleveland, Ohio. But once we step out of the X15, then relative to the garage there and the hedge we're in Feddersen's backyard."

"No one raised that question," said Gardner, "about being in Feddersen's backyard."

"It's plain relativity," I tried to get them to understand. The three of them studied me. I could've been a hole in a fence they were squinting though.

"That's all we got to remember," I pointed out. "When we're inside the X15, whether it's in the middle of China or the Sahara desert or Cleveland, Ohio, then that's where we have to be. When we're outside the car, we're in Crestview. That's only the simple fact of the matter. It's pure scientific."

"He's right there." Ray was the first on my side. "Rela-

74

tivity's nothing but science."

"Maybe so," Pete thought it over.

"Well, then no one can stop us from going around the world, not if we do it scientific," Ray pointed out.

"You got to be right there," Pete agreed. "Look at jets. Or even space capsules. They circle the globe every ninety minutes. And for only one reason, they're scientific."

"So why not us?" asked Ray.

"Except we're not in the same class." Gardner worried. "Not with capsules. We're only making it up in our minds, just thinking scientific."

"You got to start someplace," Pete argued.

"Thinking's the most important part," Ray took over. "How about Einstein? He did nothing but think. Where'd you get a bigger scientist than him?"

Gardner backed off. "I'm not saying he wasn't."

Pete kept right after him. "Then what have you got against going around the world?"

"Me? Nothing."

"Or science?" Ray forced him step by step. "What have you got against that?"

"Who's against science? You think I'm crazy?" Gardner disappeared around the corner of the car with the other two right after him.

The three of them ended up on the other side of the X15, again, arguing it out between themselves. Nervous as I was, I kept picking leaves off the hedge to chew on. Then Ray let out a yell. And I heard Pete say something about heading straight for China. And even Gardner mentioned, when all was said and done, how I was the biggest thing that happened to the X15 since they found their carburetor in

Monohan's junkyard. They came charging back then and the three of them stood in front of me.

"We decided, Henry Three," Pete did the talking, "we want you for a member in the X15." Now it was over, the long wait, I couldn't help laughing. "What's so funny?"

"Nothing. I guess, I'm glad. That's all."

"So are we," said Ray.

"Well, sure," I told them. "If you want to make me a member I wouldn't mind. How do we go about it?"

"There's no way to go about it," said Gardner. "You're just a member that's all. At least," he looked to the others, "a half-fledged member."

I had to be half-fledged, they explained, until I paid up my share of what it cost to build the X15, just for the materials. They weren't going to charge me for labor. It was going to take a dollar a week for forty-six weeks in addition, of course, to the normal running expenses like gas, oil and roadstands. Once I finished paying my share I'd be a full fledged member.

It certainly sounded fair enough, if I could raise the extra dollar a week at home.

That wasn't too much a problem. Ma and Sis knew that the X15 was about the most exclusive thing, my age, in Crestview. They were proud I was asked to join. It was generally agreed that even though Ma was a member of the Entertainment Committee of the PTA by now, and Sis had a fine collection of fellows started, and Lady was counting up to seven, and Dad was playing bridge on the train every night with Mr. Driscoll and Mr. Slattersley, that out of the whole family I was doing the best. On that basis it was easy enough getting the dollar raise I needed for my allowance.

I ACTUALLY TURNED INTO AS BIG A WHEEL ALMOST AS
Ray and Pete and Gardner. When the news came out the
X15 was traveling around the world every afternoon, I found
myself getting looked up to in a personal way. Because Ray
and Pete and Gardner gave me all the credit. They were
glad to admit that if I hadn't come along the X15 would still
be in Feddersen's backyard behind the garage.

We got hounded every morning, the four of us, with all
the kids wanting to know how far we'd traveled the day
before. I found myself walking around like a quarterback
most of the time, in the middle of a huddle, explaining how
we managed to get so far so fast.

It took us four hours to make it from Cleveland out to
San Francisco mostly by detouring the big cities and averag-
ing, while Pete kept an eye out the back window for speed

cops, better than seventy miles an hour across Wyoming. We almost got stopped by a freak snowstorm coming through the Donner Pass in California. But we had tire chains to put on and the snow ploughs showed up fast enough, according to the radio.

There was a P&O boat leaving San Francisco for Shanghai that Ray found in the shipping columns of the New York Times. They had the time listed that the boat was leaving and we made it with a half hour to spare. The next afternoon, we drove the X15 off the pier into China.

There's no question that was fast, getting the car across the Pacific Ocean in less than twenty-four hours. We wouldn't have managed if Gardner hadn't gone so whole hog for relativity. It was he who spotted some place out in the Pacific called a Date Line where you put yourself a day ahead or a day behind relative to the direction you were traveling in. Gardner figured as long as there was a Date Line that opened the door for us. Relative to our not wasting any time, he asked, why couldn't we skip the twenty-five days it took to make the trip as long as we were skipping. None of us could see why not.

Heading into China, the X15 was packed full. Most of what we had was books. Because we couldn't find any road maps of China, Ray and I borrowed five different travel books, with pictures as well as maps, from the big library there is in Bayside. Plus, we had three atlases. And finally, I brought over the twenty-four volumes of our Encyclopedia Britannica.

Besides, the car was stuffed with windbreakers, Ray's air rifle, extra water, in case of deserts, and extra rations, in case we didn't meet any roadstands.

The food we did run into, traveling from Shanghai to Soochow to Peking was pretty special. None of us had ever tried shark fins before, or thousand-year-old eggs, or fermented black beans or snake meat. But we took a chance and made believe that's what we were eating when we opened our Baby Ruths and Lorna Doones and Hershey Bars. Actually, none of it tasted too bad once you stopped thinking of the name of what you were biting into.

We saw the Great Wall of China going west at Kalgan. It was about fifteen hundred miles long and in some places thirty feet high. West of there we headed through Bayan Obo and out into the empty Gobi Desert through a town called Tingyuanying where we had to quit for the afternoon so Ray could keep a dentist appointment.

I'll never forget Tingyuanying.

It was the night we arrived there that Dad came home with his big piece of news and from then on things were never the same for us Loverings. Dad stood in the door, his arms so full of yellow roses and champagne along with his dispatch case, that he and Ma didn't manage to get much of a kiss. Dad wouldn't talk until we all got down to the playroom and each one of us had our own kind of drink poured out, waiting.

"Let me just put it this way," Dad lifted his glass. "We're in."

"You made Vice-President!" I yelled.

"Not so fast."

"Please." Ma's hand trembled but she didn't spill a drop of her champagne. "Please tell us."

"I say we're in. Isn't that enough to drink on?"

No one drank. We all rushed for Dad to hold on to and

to kiss. "Lay off," he sorted us out. "And drink up."

We had our drinks and we listened. It happened that morning in the office of Mr. Matthews, the President of A. L. & L. After a meeting, Dad described, "Mr. Matthews nodded to me and said, 'I read your proposal, Lovering'." Dad finished his champagne, waiting to hear what we thought.

"Your plan," said Sis. "He read it."

"Exactly."

"What did he have to say about it?"

"I just told you."

"That's all he had to say?"

Dad nodded. Ma and Sis and I watched him. Lady put down her chocolate milk and wiped away the mustache.

"You'd think," Sis spoke up, "he'd say something more. You know, whether he liked it."

"Matthews?" Dad walked to the bar holding his head at the pain of having such a stupid family. "Oh, brother, aren't you people ever going to learn? It's a hundred to one for any report to ever reach the top at American Lock and Locomotive. If it does Matthews doesn't have to tell you whether he likes it or not. He doesn't even have to tell you whether he's read it. He doesn't have to commit himself in any way whatsoever. But if he does, if he mentions it, that's Bingo. The lights go on. You're in!"

"Do you really think," my mother asked, "that's the way it is, Dad?"

"I don't have to think. Mac was with me. Soon as we left the office, Mac opened up. 'You made it,' he said."

"Well praise be, Mac ought to know. Long as he's been first vice-president to Matthews." Ma raised her glass.

"Major Henry Lovering, Junior, let me be the first to congratulate you."

Ma got to Dad first as the rest of us closed in again. Dad lifted her off the floor. It was hard to pry them apart for any one to be the second to congratulate Dad. And from then on we laughed at how wonderful we were turning out to be. That was the biggest moment for us Loverings in all the years I can remember, at two minutes to seven o'clock on the night we reached Tingyuanying.

Then the phone rang and it was Gardner. He sounded choked. "Henry Three!"

"Speaking," I said.

"For Heaven sakes, Henry Three," he yelled.

"You're talking to him."

His voice went higher. "Wait'll you hear?"

"Aw come on, Gardner. What's up?"

"In two minutes on Channel Four."

"What?"

"On the seven o'clock news."

"Well look, Gardner," I told him. "I'll go see what it is and call you back."

No one wanted T.V. but they stopped to watch when the announcer came on. He looked very solemn. He had a report from the People's Republic of China announcing how they'd set off, the day before, the first Chinese Hydrogen Bomb. The announcer went on to tell us that the next morning the People's Republic was going to start testing a whole series of bombs, big ones, out in the Gobi Desert.

"But we were talking about furniture," said Sis. "Do we have to listen?"

"Hold it, Sister," Dad put down his glass. "Let's hear this."

The commentator read where the People's Republic, in the interest of world peace, wanted everyone to know the exact location of the test that was starting in the morning. He walked over to a map to show us. It was the same map of the Gobi Desert I'd been looking at all afternoon in the encyclopedia! And right in the middle, one of the towns that was getting evacuated, was where we'd parked the X15 for the night. Tingyuanying! No wonder Gardner was lock-jawed. The X15 was going up in smoke!

"The People's Republic offers visual evidence of the first detonation which occurred yesterday afternoon." The commentator looked to one side of the television set and the screen went white.

And then the roar began while the picture tube looked like it was folding in on itself to show the shape of an atom bomb growing up lazy and slow, turning its insides out and climbing to a stop that reached higher again while inside the fog a faint circle of the sun began to hatch and grow brighter, forcing its way through the ring of clouds that gently rose as the white hot sun stood sure and bright and growing until it filled the twenty-one inch screen with glitter to sprout, suddenly, another cyclone shooting higher still that spread a slow smoke wave which hung there, dead and still and cold. Our playroom was filled with the thunder of it.

I slid for the phone and started dialing.

"What's come over you?" asked Sis.

Gardner's line was busy. So was Ray's. I dialed Pete. "This is serious," I told Sis.

"It's that all right." Dad went over and turned off the TV. "There's been talk of this coming through the office."

He seemed shocked as I was. Slowly he sat down on the couch. "I never thought we'd have to face it so soon," he told Ma.

Pete's line was busy. I hung up. The phone rang. It was Gardner. "Everyone's phone is busy," he said.

"Because we're all dialing each other."

"Did you hear him?" yelled Gardner. "They're going to blast the X15."

"We got to get it out of there."

"And right this minute. I'll see you at Pete's."

"I'm coming," I hung up. The phone rang. It was Ray.

"Where are you coming?" asked Ma.

"We're moving the X15 out," I told her.

"At least five hundred miles," Ray answered me on the phone.

"But not without your dinner," said Ma.

"I'll have my dinner later."

"Me too," Ray shouted over the wire.

"But Henry, you can't rush off without eating just because the Chinese dropped a bomb."

"We can't let them wipe out the X15, can we?"

"Over my dead body," yelled Ray. "Come on, Henry, we're high tailing out of there!" He hung up leaving me with the phone to my ear, trying to explain it all to my mother. "We won't drive further than India," I promised.

"Now listen," Ma started but Dad nodded for her to give me permission. I dashed for the stairs. "But not too late," said Ma. "And Hank!" I turned. "Where are you taking that?" I looked at the phone in my hand. I had to go back and hang it up before I ran.

When I made it to Pete's the others were stowing away

sandwiches that Mrs. Feddersen fixed up, plus a two quart thermos of hot chocolate and last, a dozen doughnuts.

We pulled away from Tingyuanying. The road turned the wrong way, to the north. Every turn was to the right. There was no way to go except deeper into the Gobi desert. We were trapped. In a couple hours the whole country was getting charred to a cinder.

We dug into every book we had. It was Ray saved us. He found one written by an Englishman in 1888. Under the flashlight the book showed a caravan route for camels, that turned left. It went south, away from the Gobi Desert. We raced for the turn and headed south at five miles an hour, which is what we estimated a camel might average.

It was rough. We came up against the highest mountains in the world, the Himalayas. We detoured east, into Tibet. Even so we got up to eight thousand feet. We traveled along a gorge, according to that 1888 book, that dropped a quarter mile below us. Gardner hung out the window with a flashlight to keep us from the edge of the road. We were lucky. We came through all right.

We kept going until we put about four hundred and seventy miles between the X15 and the Chinese test site in the Gobi desert. We pulled into a town in Tibet called Kokoshili, population—8700, products—goat cheese. It was there we quit for the night. We were plenty weary. And plenty safe enough, that's what I thought, so we could forget the hydrogen bomb.

8

ACTUALLY, I NEVER DID GET MY MIND MADE UP ABOUT the atom bomb. Even though it's been around all my life, there's not much to it you can think about. Besides Boom! Or maybe a city that all of a sudden turns into a stretch of nothing but piled-up empty lots. That's about as far as I ever got, imagining an atom bomb.

And for sure I never did see myself getting mixed up with one of them in a private way, when it was something I had to worry about just on my own. Because there's this about an atom bomb, no matter how terrible it is there's nothing personal to it. You can't get hit with one unless sixty or seventy square miles of neighbors blow up at the same time. So it's nothing that you personally have to lose any sleep over. That's what I thought.

The Chinese bombs, though, didn't work that way. Once they started exploding in the Gobi desert, they almost wiped us out. I mean just us, the Loverings. They were the worst thing ever happened to our family.

As far as the rest of Crestview went no one seemed particularly interested in the Chinese, whatever they were cooking up. To everyone else it was only another international crisis, the kind where the President comes on T.V. and says the future of the world is at stake. And then the different channels put on those panel shows where four or five men sit around interrupting each other. That's what happened this time, and no one around hardly even mentioned it.

Except at our house. That's all they could talk about, my mother and Dad. The next four or five days what we had for dinner and far into the night was the Chinese hydrogen bomb and whether it was going to mean peace or war. And when the two of them weren't hashing that over or reading the newspapers through or watching the special shows on T.V., Dad was back at the dinning room table again, working. He started to put in longer hours during those nights than even for his reorganization plan.

And when he finally did come home and give each of us his new business card that actually said on it *Vice-President,* the night I always thought we'd have our biggest celebration, neither Dad nor Ma gave it much notice. Dad spread his papers on the dining room table as usual and then went off for a quick nap before getting down to work.

"How come?" I tried to find out from Ma.

"You'd think," said Sis, "the atom bomb was a family affair, our own special problem."

"It is in a way," Ma told us. "It's part of your father's new job."

"Bombs?"

"How to protect ourselves from them," Ma nodded. "That's what your father's up to." When Dad made Vice-President, Ma described, he was put in charge of the Zero Division of A. L. & L. That was a part of the company that made products for survival, different items you'd need for when the countdown reaches zero. Most of the things were for underground installations built by the government or the army. But the Zero Division was all equipped to turn out bomb shelters, if they were ever needed, for families as well.

That's why Dad was so wrapped up with the international crisis. He had to figure if the public was taking it serious enough, the chance for war, to start an actual market for family type bomb shelters. It was Dad's first big step as Vice-President, whether to recommend for A.L. & L. to start selling shelters or not. The final decision of course was up to the President of the company, Mr. Matthews, but Dad's whole future depended on the recommendation he thought up.

I didn't dream the hydrogen bomb was that serious, where it could mess things up for our family. Dad tried to handle the deal as careful as he could. Ma described how he was conducting a survey of what people thought along with setting up test shelters all over the country to get reactions. It wasn't clear yet what Dad was going to recommend but meanwhile he was getting everything ready in case things took a turn for the worst.

Ma showed us the sales campaign that Dad had worked out. There were selling manuals and advertisements and even a letter Dad wrote for Mr. Matthews, the President, to fill a whole page in the newspaper. It explained how Mr. Matthews' deepest hope was for a practical way to stop wars that A. L. & L. could support to the limit. Until that showed up though, Mr. Matthews thought a bomb shelter was like any other kind of insurance.

"A. L. & L. offers this product," Mr. Matthews' letter read, "not because we think you'll need it tomorrow, next week or next year. We know as little about that as you do. Our survival unit is offered on the same basis as a life insurance policy for the contribution it makes, today, to your peace of mind from now on."

It made all the difference to Sis and me, what Ma told us. It was a cinch to see now what a headache China was turning out to be for Dad. But serious as it was, what really caught our eye in Dad's campaign was the sales brochure. All in color, it showed three different types of bomb shelters, the Home Zero, the Family Zero and the Super Zero.

Sis couldn't get over the Super Zero. "It's even sort of cute," was what she thought. "Imagine an early American bomb shelter."

"Personally," said Ma, "I can't. But how would you like to have one?"

"Who?" asked Sis. "Us?"

"One of our own?" I looked at Ma.

My mother nodded and Sis was off like a shot, running on about bomb-proof parties and the friends she could put up in the shelter for house guests. "We'd be the first ones in Crestview. There's lots have swimming pools. There's even two tennis courts. But a bomb shelter, that'd top them all."

"Could we?" I asked. "I mean have one?"

"I'm afraid we can't avoid it," Ma sighed. "The thought occured to Mr. Matthews that your Dad might have one of the test shelters installed out here. So he might study it in an actual home situation. And that's that. Whatever occurs to Mr. Matthews ends up the law. They're shipping one out."

"No!" Sis lost her breath. "When?"

"In two or three days."

Sis grabbed for my mother. "What could be lovelier?"

I couldn't help agree.

"I hope you're right," Ma smiled at us. "Because there's nothing we can do to stop it from coming."

Our class was deep breathing when it did show up. So it had to be about ten in the morning. That's the time Dokstra usually gets us to our feet facing the glass windows where the air conditioners are and, while we look out across the lawn to the streets below, she counts, "One, two, three In. One, two, three Out."

Miss Dokstra had just finished with "In", when around the corner ambled a long flatbed trailer truck that had to be thirty feet or more. On the back was a bulldozer with a scoop shovel attached. But most of what you saw was this big, gleaming steel section of a tunnel that looked like a solid chunk out of the middle of an airliner. Across the middle it was lettered, SUPER ZERO BOMB SHELTER.

The rig climbed slow up the hill, crawling left to right across the window we were all looking through.

Miss Dokstra said, "One, two, three, Out." But you didn't hear any exhale. The whole class watched the strung out trailer make a lazy left turn into the quiet streets of Crestview and disappear.

89

"One, two, three, Out." Miss Dokstra repeated. And everyone's breath when it came was a rush of talk that filled the room. The bomb shelter had to be going to someone in Crestview, was everyone's question, else it wouldn't be off the highway. Who? The whole class pointed at each other and everyone shook their heads, except me. I was glad to admit it belonged to us.

Miss Dokstra had to lay on to her desk with a yard rule to quiet the excitement. And all that morning I could've been Montgomery Ward, the mail that came in. Everyone

sent me notes asking how about it, would I let them into the bomb shelter to see what it was like?

By the last bell the Super Zero had turned into the biggest thing in Crestview, bigger even than the X15. Ray and Pete and Gardner were as anxious as everyone else to get a look at a real modern survival unit. None of the three mentioned the importance that came my way all of a sudden, just on my own. They cancelled leaving Calcutta that afternoon, where we happened to be, and joined the mob at the bike rack waiting for me to take them home. The stream of kids that set off from school, every bike racing down the hill, looked like there was a fire.

It was a surprise to find the Super Zero practically installed. Even though I'd read in Dad's manual how that was its big feature; it was an all-in packaged unit that had only to be lowered into a hole in the ground. By the time the crowd of us showed up the Super Zero was covered with dirt and the men on the job were laying out the rolled up sod to make the lawn look as good as it was.

Our backyard could have been a convention. Ma had a lot of ladies visiting. And along with the workmen, there were four junior executives from Dad's office checking things with stop watches and cameras and notebooks. Sis had brought a crowd from High School and we were forced to wait until they came up from the shelter before there was any room for us.

I was as much bowled over by the Super Zero as everyone else, by the double decker bunks and the extra crib there was for Lady, the sealed up pantry where the survival rations didn't have to be replaced except every two years, the filtered air intake that worked off its own electric generator and the medical cabinet that had everything from plastic splints for a broken leg to special pills you took if, for any reason, you felt sad. It was all complete.

Shep Untermeyer's dog, Winner, curled up in one of the bunks. "I don't blame him," said Al Sommers. "It'd be real solid, better than a vacation, surviving in a place like this."

You couldn't help agree what a kick it would be if a chance ever did come along to actually use the Super Zero. It was a feeling built up with everything you looked at, like the different instruments there were for measuring radioactive roentgens. I read out of the Owner's Manual, "Your new all-in survival unit resists twenty psi over-pressure which is equal to six miles from ground zero of a twenty megaton detonation." Whatever that meant, we were all scared into laughing. But it was Conelrad that started it.

The Owner's Manual said, "Once you hear an attack alert, which is a steady siren that goes from three to five minutes, tune your radio to Conelrad, six forty on your dial." Gardner let out a rumbling screech that built up into a scream and Winner, waking up, joined in until the two of them sounded perfect as an air raid siren. Pete read the sample radio announcement out of the Manual, "This is Station WJZ. In cooperation with Civil Defense measures as requested by the United States Government, normal broadcasting is now discontinued for an indefinite period. This is a Conelrad Radio Alert. Tune immediately to your Conelrad frequency for further instructions."

By then, all of us had dived into the bunks and some underneath, real as it felt. Pete went on, making the rest up out of his head. "Hello folks. This is your friendly Conelrad reporter. And let me tell you we've got a real exciting program coming up."

Pete described how we were attacked by three giant hydrogen missiles coming in off the Pacific that were headed for New York and went on about radar and computers until you almost believed him. Chuck Driscoll started a countdown that began with one hundred.

Sommers didn't see why we just had to sit there and take it. He turned the Super Zero into an anti-missile missile base somewhere in Kansas and knocked down one of the atom bombs. Arnie Untermeyer came up with the idea we were a Polaris submarine at the North Pole. He hung on to the air intake valve to use as a periscope and kept yelling "Achtung" until someone reminded him that it was German. With the help of a couple of others, Arnie managed to launch a couple of bombs back at the enemy.

At times it got confusing. The yelling went on; you couldn't tell whether we were Conelrad Control, or Anti-Missile Missile, or Polaris, or what. Al Sommers and Gardner took a couple of pokes at each other, in the excitement, to decide what was happening. Pete, though, managed to take over as his hydrogen bombs closed in on New York City. Everyone joined in on the countdown. "Five, four, three, two, ONE!" And then we all let go while Chuck hauled off at the empty water tank that added a base-drum effect to the explosion. It was loud enough to tear the roof out of the Super Zero if there hadn't been three feet of dirt piled on top.

We finished up winded. Ma knocked just about then, wanting to bring some of her ladies down. And trooping out of the place, most of the crowd agreed there was a lot of sport to having your own bomb shelter. Practically everyone wanted to come back whenever I'd let them for another workout, and some even asked if they could spend the night. It began to look as if a bomb shelter might be almost as popular an idea around Crestview as a cabin cruiser or a swimming pool. Especially, everyone could see, if it ever happened that a bomb did get dropped for real.

"But then," it was Arnie's kid brother Shep who asked that question first, "if there is a bomb, what happens to the rest of us?"

9

IT WAS A DIVIDING LINE, SHEP'S QUESTION, THAT GREW wider and wider in the days to come. On one side was us Loverings and on the other was all the rest of Crestview.

Even the next morning you could feel a difference, as if a change of season had come to town. No one mentioned getting back to the Super Zero for the fun it was. No one brought up the bomb shelter at all, not to me, except to check how much it cost, or how thick were the walls. And then he'd go back, whoever asked me, to a bunch of the others that were talking it over.

I began to get the feeling that the only conversation the next couple of days around school and over everyone's dinner at home, was us Loverings and our survival unit. Before I knew it, Crestview made its mind up. And then it came at me in a dozen different ways, the question that started with Shep.

"Where do you and your family come off?" Chuck Driscoll asked me. We were crowded into a booth down at Pirelli's Pharmacy, and all the others nodded. "What makes you think you're so special?"

"In what connection?" I waited to find out. "No one around our house thinks we're special."

"Then how come you're fixing to be the only ones to survive?"

"If a bomb does drop," Al Sommers pointed out.

"Where'd you get that idea?" I laughed but none of them joined in. "Our Super Zero's not the only one there is. Anyone can buy a bomb shelter."

"Who wants one?" said Chuck. "You won't catch us crawling into any hole in the ground, no matter what."

"Then of course." All I wanted was to agree with him. "If that's how you feel, you can skip it. No one's forcing you to get one."

"You are," Al pointed a spoon of chocolate ice cream. "You putting in that shelter, that's as much as to say the rest of us are fools for not trying to protect ourselves."

"Not at all. You got us all wrong, Al." I picked a toothpick out of the holder on the table and broke it into smaller and smaller bits. "Look, you fellows, this whole thing's only a business proposition, that's all, up at my Dad's office. That's the only reason we got a Super Zero."

"That's even worse," said Chuck. "If you take atom bombs serious enough you go into business."

"No one's ever going to start dropping atom bombs," Mike Buell agreed with Driscoll. "He has to be off his rocker to take them that serious."

"Who? My father?" It wasn't that I wanted to start any arguments, not in Crestview, just over a difference of opinion. But I couldn't let a remark like that go by, not about Dad. "Maybe some of you ought to find out if maybe they are serious."

"How?"

"I'll show you." I left them, sliding past the bent straws and the broken toothpicks in the puddles on the table. I found the clipping I wanted in Dad's collection of papers and I brought it out for a crowd of them at school next day, during lunch.

"A single nuclear weapon," I read, "can release more destructive energy than all the explosives used in all the wars in history." I looked at Mike Buell. "That sounds serious enough, doesn't it?"

"Well," admitted Buell.

I read some more. "The world's nuclear stockpile today contains, it is estimated, the equivalent of thirty billion tons of TNT, about ten tons of TNT for every human being on the globe. Our scientists tell us that radioactive fallout from a single bomb can wipe out all higher forms of life in an area of 10,000 square miles."

"From a single bomb?" asked Arnie Untermeyer.

"Just one bomb. And listen to this," I finished the clipping. "No wonder it has been bitterly said that life on other planets may be extinct because their scientists were more advanced than ours."

"Well, that shows you," said Al Sommers. "The guy who wrote that is a crackpot. Anyone who'd make that kind of remark about scientists. So how can you believe some of those figures he gives you?"

"Crackpot?" I let Al read the clipping himself. "You call John F. Kennedy a crackpot?"

"Kennedy said that, the one who was President?"

"This is what he said even before he got to be President. So it can't help but be a lot worse now."

Someone let out a whistle and the whole crowd looked startled enough. I wasn't out to win arguments. I wanted nothing from any of them except they forget the bomb shelter and let things be. So they'd keep on being friends of mine. But the questions kept coming.

"If one bomb is bigger than all the wars in history," Ray Sattersley asked me, "what's the use of any shelter? How can it save you?"

The four of us were traveling through Arabia that afternoon on our way in the X15 from Karachi to Bagdad. I was the one looking up Bagdad and there seemed a lot around town worth seeing. The last thing I wanted was to go on anymore about the shelter. But the three of them twisted my way, while Pete cut the motor, looking for an answer. I had to put the encyclopedia I was reading, *AUS to CAL*, back on the pile next to me.

"All it gives us is a little peace of mind," I remembered the advertisement Dad wrote for the President of A. L. & L. "It's like insurance. The insurance you buy doesn't keep you from dying. It only gives you a feeling of security. Same thing with a bomb shelter. There's the security you feel just having one around."

"Where's the security," said Ray, "if it can't help when you get hit with all the wars in history? You got to be dim-witted to buy a shelter, my old man says, to throw your money away like that."

It was warm down there in the middle of Arabia. It smelled sour from how warm it was and I wiped the damp from my upper lip. "Well," I took a chance explaining, "suppose there's no direct hit. At least it comes in handy for the radioactive part. A shelter protects you from fall-out which doesn't last more than two or three weeks. After that you can come out again."

"To see what?" asked Pete. "None of us'll be around. We're not buying any shelter."

"Us neither," said Gardner. "My father thinks if the people around here are good enough to live with, they're good enough to get killed with. If we have to go, we all go together."

"That's only natural," agreed Ray. "Unless you think you're better than everyone else around here."

. "For heaven's sake," I tried to get them to see. "The way you talk you'd think it was us Loverings who invented the atom bomb and nuclear and all."

"You're the ones who brought it up," said Gardner.

"We brought it up! It's only in all the papers and on T.V."

"So's murder," Pete mentioned. "Is that any reason to bring it into Crestview?"

I gave up. As if there was any use talking. The best thing was get back to Arabia, the four of us, but when I reached for the encyclopedia Gardner shook his head. "Bagdad's too far up the line for me, this afternoon anyway."

"Me too," Pete opened the door.

Ray slid out after him. "Here's where we get off then."

We stepped out and though it had happened dozens of

times before, I never noticed how the three of them headed in one direction and I went in another. I was scared. It was slipping away. Every decent thing we'd found in Crestview, me and my family, we were starting to lose.

Until losing became a part of whatever went on. There's even a color to losing. It's brown, like the one dead leaf on a full green tree is brown, twisting slow and waiting to drop. And the smell of losing is sour as a dirty T-shirt the morning after a ball game. There's a taste to it, too, that's dry and salty. You could be running a temperature, the way losing tastes. And the sound of it is far off. Losing is an echo of all the noises you pass through while you think only of what's wrong. It's brittle, losing, like the feel of toothpicks you snap between your fingers in Pirelli's Pharmacy, trying to answer questions. And then the way I kept losing, there was no more chance left even to answer questions.

We were riding home from school, some of us, through the shining streets still wet from the morning's shower when Shep Untermeyer came pedaling up behind us.

"Hey you, Three!" he yelled. "Can I come over and stay with you when the bomb drops?"

"Sure." We stopped in front of the Untermeyers'. "Anytime," I answered Shep. "You've got a standing invitation."

"No he hasn't." His big brother Arnie stopped me from answering. "Didn't I tell you last night," he reminded Shep, "they only got room for five. They can't take you even if they wanted."

"Who needs so much room?" asked Shep. "Not me."

"It's not only the size of the place," Arnie yelled at the red head. "They only got enough air, food and water for their own family down there."

"Just a second." I wasn't going to let Arnie take over. "He asked me, didn't he? And I'm telling you, Shep, we'd be glad to have you."

"No you can't," Chuck Driscoll stopped me. "The thing is, you'd have to shoot him."

"Who, Shep?" I laughed. "That's crazy."

"No it isn't. If a bomb does drop it's practically your bounden duty to shoot anyone who tries to get in with you, in your own bomb shelter. According to my Ma."

"How does she know?"

"She got it from this Reverend she was reading about, up at Georgetown University. The religious thing is to protect your own family first, once you got them safe in their shelter. It's your duty to keep your neighbors out. Down at Princeton, too, there's a Father who says the same thing."

"Where the ones in the bomb shelter have a right to shoot you?" asked Arnie.

Chuck nodded at me. "He'd have to, that's all."

They looked at me, the crowd of them, like I was the enemy. It was dry to swallow and there wasn't anything I had to say anyway. They were the ones, now, who were coming up with all the answers. They hurried away, Arnie and Chuck and the rest of them, and I was alone except for Shep.

"Is it a rifle?" he asked. "The gun you got? Or a western kind?" He drew from an imaginary holster.

"You don't have to believe any of that," I told him. "We'd never shoot you, not you Shep. Honest."

"Even if you did, I'd know you couldn't help it." Shep

looked around to where Winner, at a window, was barking for him to come home. "So I'm not mad." He took off down the driveway.

Riding alone, and not listening except to all the worst things that came to mind, I didn't hear Shep again. He yelled for me to stop. He caught me at the corner of his block.

"I just thought." Shep was out of breath. "He's different."

"Who is?"

"Winner. He's a dog. You know Winner. He don't eat so much. And he hardly breathes any air at all. I'm not asking about me. Just Winner. I mean if the bomb comes."

"For us to take Winner down into the shelter?"

"You wouldn't have to shoot a dog, would you?"

"I guess not." You couldn't help notice the lawn that stretched away, wet and green and crowded with leaves shook loose by the wind and the rain, they were dead leaves mostly brown.

"Then how about it?" Shep touched my wrist. "Is there any chance you could save Winner for me?"

"I think so," I turned back to him. "I promise you Shep. Cross my heart. Whatever happens we'll take care of Winner."

Shep let out a high yell and took off. So at least there was someone in Crestview who was happy about our bomb shelter, one redheaded second grader pedaling down the wet pavement with good news for his dog.

10

CONSIDERING HOW DAD IS MOSTLY TIED UP WITH HIS OWN troubles at the office, it's our mother who usually handles what's wrong with the family. By now there was plenty for her to handle. I yelled for Ma once I closed the kitchen door behind me. No one answered. There was the sound though like a catch in the plumbing, a sort of moaning filled with hiccups. I traced it through the living room down the hall to Sis's room. She was stretched across the bed, her black-and-white shoes dangling over the side and the tail of brown hair tossed up on the pillow, crying.

"Where's Ma?" I asked her.

"Go away," she said into the blue and yellow bars of the bedspread.

"Just is she in or not, is all I want to know."

"Imbecile!" Sis bounced on the mattress.

103

"Take it easy, Sis. What did I do?"

"He's the imbecile. Warren Andrews."

I got the picture then. "You had a fight." She crawled up into her hair on the pillow and sounded like a dying balloon. "And I bet I know what it's about. The bomb shelter."

Sis collected her hair to one side and looked at me. Her face could've been a washed shirt that needed ironing. "Henry, it's awful."

"It's about time Ma did something about it."

There was a scream like someone falling out of a twenty story window. It came up again and then settled into a watery wail that broke, every so often, into a howl. It was Lady downstairs and there's where Ma had to be.

The playroom was set up for a party with plates and sandwiches spread around the Ping-Pong table along with pitchers of milk. Mom was wearing new slacks, dark blue, and Lady had on the kind of uniform Brownies wear, except it was red, with a beret. She was sitting on Ma's knee getting jiggled to the tune of *"I got sixpence, jolly, jolly sixpence."* From the way Lady took on, it didn't sound like it was her kind of number.

Ma shook Lady's chin and pointed. "Look at the funny monkey. Go ahead, Henry. Get up and walk on your hands."

It worked, the way it usually did. After I padded around a bit, Lady turned herself off to no more than a gurgle. Then she laughed. "Funny monkey," she pointed at me.

"And now we're going to have a party all by ourselves." Ma gave Lady a cookie and filled the glasses with milk. "Drinks for everybody."

"Who needs milk?" asked Sis.

Ma put a glass in her hand. "You drink up. And enjoy it. Lady's got to have some kind of a party."

"I wanna march." Lady juggled her glass back on the table. Ma wiped a dribble off the side of her mouth.

"Here we go!" Ma came out with that tune again and we made it around the Ping-Pong table hitting the heavy beat with our right foot. Lady picked up the count and yelled it off in numbers that went all the way up to nine, which was a surprise to me she could get that far.

"What's this all about?" asked Sis.

"We're inaugurating the Lady Bugs of America this afternoon, sort of a pre-Brownie organization." Ma described how seven mothers had been due to bring their little girls but five phoned they couldn't make it. So Ma called the whole thing off.

"You know why," said Sis. "Why they couldn't make it, don't you?"

"March, march," Lady lunged at Sis and pushed her back into step.

"Yes Sis, I know why." Ma pounded around the table.

Sis held to a corner. "Then what are we going to do about it?"

"I don't know," my mother said. "Just keep moving. Go on."

That only had to be a way of talking, for my mother to say she didn't know. "You just haven't thought it over." I said, "about the bomb shelter. That's all you mean. You haven't figured it out yet."

The hair my mother has is the lightish kind about the color of a natural finished baseball bat. Circling the other side of the table Ma wiped it back from her forehead. "I've thought, Henry Three. I've thought about very little else these past few days."

"Then you can see we're getting ruined for good," Sis came up behind her, "less you fix it."

"I'd certainly like to, Sis, but I'm not at all sure that I can."

Sis wailed. "Then what's going to happen?" She tossed herself into the couch like she was a handful of waste paper and tried to smother herself in the pillow.

"Sister, sister." Ma went to the floor, kneeling beside her. "That's not going to help." She tried to get the head free, at least, so Sis could breathe.

I sat down on the coffee table. "But if you don't know what to do, then what happens?"

Ma held my knee. "Take it easy, Henry Three."

"I'm okay."

Ma checked Lady who was carrying on practically automatic by now, yelling her numbers around the table. "Listen you two," she dug Sis out of the pillow. "I know how bad this is. So does your Dad. We've had dates broken, dinner invitations canceled. It's been very bad for us. And there's no way to handle it. We can't talk this thing away or apologize it out of existence. It's something we're going to have to weather through, that's all, and keep hoping for a change. And hysterics won't help."

Lady screamed. She came out of the stamping trance she was in to find herself the only one in the parade. "March!" she pulled at Ma. "You!" she butted me. Then she gave up and bellowed out a storm.

"Baby, baby." Ma folded the girl in her lap and looked

around at the three of us. "You know what we're going to do?" she kissed Lady quietly. "I've ordered some beautiful flowers to plant. Yellow ones and red ones." She lifted me up by the back of the neck. "Come on you two." She hauled Sis off the couch.

Out in the backyard there were a half dozen pots of asters in full bloom. When I brought the garden tools from the garage I saw what Ma's idea was. She wanted the plants dug in around the two pipes from the shelter that stuck up in the lawn, the air intake and the exhaust.

"What's the use hiding the pipes?" complained Sis. "Who's that going to fool?"

"No one. They're unsightly. It will get them out of the way. And next spring the planting will be attractive here on the lawn."

"If we're still here by next spring," said Sis.

"Please, no more of that." Ma loosened the earth in a pot while Lady studied the flowers. "It's nice to be a Lady Bug," said Lady.

I stamped the spade into the ground. "There's only one thing to do. Let's get rid of the Super Zero. Give it back. Get it out of here."

"We can't. It's still part of your Daddy's job, Henry."

"And don't think," Sis put in, "everybody doesn't go on about it. Warren talks like Dad was Boris Karloff, Frankenstein."

"That's interesting," Ma straightened. "In what way?"

"He says the more people Dad can frighten, the more money he makes. Warren says if there's a good war scare Dad stands to clean up a fortune."

"Does he though? And what do you think, sister?"

"What difference does it make what I think?"

"You're the important one." Ma pointed her handrake at Sis. "The last thing I'm going to let this shelter do is create any misunderstanding about your own father. Whatever Warren says, Dad's no different from any other man in this town."

"You don't have to tell me, Ma."

"But I am Sis. And I want to make it very clear." Ma tucked the rake under her arm and tapped her pinkie. "I don't know very much about business. But I've never heard of a big corporation, the kind these men work for, that didn't have the government for one of its best customers. Or the Army. Or the Navy. There's never a cocktail party you don't run into talk about defense contracts. So it isn't only your father. His job doesn't have any more to do with war than any of the rest of them."

"Don't I know?" said Sis. "It wasn't my idea."

"Then it'll be that much easier for you to forget it." Ma took her rake again. "And you too, Hank."

"Sure," I promised. "But even if everybody here is in the war business, can't Dad get out of the Super Zero part. So we can send the thing back. After all," I pointed out, "there's hardly any international crisis left on T.V."

"It has quieted down." Ma waved Lady away from picking at the asters and started back to digging. "For the moment. Even so, Mr. Matthews wants your father to keep right on with his plans. He thinks A. L. & L. ought to stay ready for whatever turns up. And from what I gather, Mr. Matthews has a mind that is very hard to change."

"But there has to be some way," I kneeled beside her,

"some way, Ma, to make him see different, all the trouble we're in."

"Please, Henry, it's beyond me." Ma pointed over the Simpsons' hedge where far away you could just see the tallest buildings in New York. "I can't change what goes on up there, in those offices. I wait, that's all, for the word to come down and then I try to live with it as best we can."

"There was that advertisement, though," I reminded Ma. "Mr. Matthews said if he knew of a good way to stop wars, there wouldn't have to be any shelters. Wouldn't that be one way to change his mind?"

"How?"

"If you'd work out some good way to stop wars."

"Me? Henry child, isn't there any limit to what you think I can do?"

"I don't mean you only. Me for instance, suppose I did."

"Well, why don't you just go ahead and do that, Henry. You think up a good, practical way to stop wars and I'll get the rest of these flowers in."

"Okay," I stood up. "I will. I'll start thinking right now."

"Fine," Sis groaned. "That's going to be a big help."

"At least it gives us something to think about. Instead of doing nothing. And what if an idea does come along to stop wars, our problem's solved."

"That'd solve a lot of problems," Ma smiled at me. "And it shouldn't be too hard to figure out, not for a youngster who can manage to go around the world in a parked automobile."

"The X15?" I checked my watch. "I better get going. We're pulling into Bagdad this afternoon."

There was the zing of a bike bell. It was the three of

them, Ray and Pete and Gardner, coming to look for me instead. They coasted up our driveway and in the wire baskets on their handle bars, I could see our encyclopedias. Each one carried a stack. The three of them stopped.

"Bad news," said Ray. "The X15 is out of commission."

Gardner said, "It's not running."

"We blew a gasket," said Pete.

"Is that serious?" I wanted to know.

"Well, to begin with," said Pete, "we have to find the part."

"And then we have to put it in," said Gardner.

"That'll take time," said Ray. "We thought only the full-fledged members, we ought to do the job ourselves."

"Well sure," I said. "You're the ones who built it in the first place."

We stood looking at each other waiting for what came next, the three of them sitting on their bikes and on our side Ma, Sis, Lady and me.

"So we thought," Gardner started up, "seeing how we won't be traveling for a while, you had your books in the car."

"We thought you might want them at home," said Ray.

"Case there was something you wanted to look up," mentioned Gardner.

"Well sure," I said. "You never know when that could happen."

"So where will we put them?" asked Pete.

"Over there's good enough, on the kitchen step."

They stacked them neat, in alphabetical order.

"Tough luck." Gardner got back on his bike. "The way things work out."

"Well a gasket," I made the remark. "It's not your fault."

We watched them pedal down the driveway and turn into the street, out of sight.

"Do you think," I asked Ma, "they blew a gasket?"

"No," Ma said.

11

WHEN I WOKE UP THE NEXT MORNING IT FELT FAMILIAR. And then I knew why. It was the same as if I were back in Seattle or Berkeley or Easton. I was back on my own again, from all I could see.

Only in those other places I never did get to have a crowd that I ran with, or some X15 to belong to, and for sure I was never any kind of wheel before I came to Crestview. Before, I never had anything to lose. The way it was now, it could be a lot worse than anything I'd ever run into. I wasn't so anxious to find out how much worse.

From my bed, you got a pretty good view of the asters we planted in our backyard. They brought up what I had to think about, how to stop wars. It looked to be a fine morning for that, to stay in bed and think.

I concentrated on my nose for a while, then on my ears

and my stomach. Usually when you concentrate on one part of you hard enough it can get an ache started or even a pretty good pain. They weren't any help, my nose, ears and stomach. But my chest, once I put my mind to it, seemed likely. And bearing down, taking one rib at a time, a weight did start building up that could be serious. It was even getting hard to breathe and I was just on the point of yelling for Ma, when Ma yelled instead.

"Not another word, Sis," I heard Ma down the hall. "That's enough of that. You're getting up and you're going to school."

Sis was working on the same deal I was, with her left leg. It ruined us both.

I rode the long way around to school. Down Havenhurst, the way I usually go, I'd run into Arnie Untermeyer and that gang who'd only get in the way of all the thinking I had to do. Even so I was early. There was a mob waiting up on the gravel driveway for the first bell.

Instead of running into all that talk, I scouted around for some place quiet where I could keep on turning over whatever came to mind. I headed for a concrete shed that was a bus stop down the street. It looked lonely enough. But when I pulled into it someone was there and my front wheel caught as I tried to twist away. I had to land on my feet to make a quick stop.

It was Fletcher Larkin. It was a surprise to see him. But he was no one you had to mind. With Fletcher Larkin, after all, nothing was changed and there was nothing to lose. He sat writing on a yellow pad and it wasn't that he smiled when he saw me, except his face got a little wider.

"Henry Three!" he put down his pad.

"I didn't know anyone was here."

"No one ever is. You wouldn't want a better place to finish your homework." He looked around the shed and laughed. "Than the Fletcher Larkin Memorial Study Hall."

"I didn't mean to bust in on you." I pulled the bike back.

"No problem. The fact is, I've been thinking to talk to you one of these days. To ask you, you know, how you like it here in Crestview?"

"It's all right," I told him. "I like it fine."

"You still feel that way? Well look," Fletch put his books together and squared them up on the concrete bench. "If you folks figure on staying here, mind if I give you a tip?"

"Go ahead."

"That air raid shelter you got. Not that I don't think it's a great idea for this place. But it's killing you. You better get rid of it."

"That's what I'm doing." It was a relief talking to Fletcher Larkin, easy as it was. He knew the worst about me anyway. And it was good to relax for once, just to have a conversation without taking apart the looks you got, just to listen to the words instead of a guy's tone of voice. As long as he was there to talk to, I got to telling Fletch about Dad and A. L. & L. and the plan I was thinking up for Mr. Matthews, so he'd take the shelter back.

"You have to find some way to stop wars?" Fletch shook his head. "Fat chance of that."

I certainly appreciated the interest he took. "Why?" I asked him.

"There was always wars."

"There was always horse and wagons too," I pointed

out, "until some one came up with a better idea."

"Well as far as that goes," Fletch admitted. "And the fact is, you're smart. Maybe you'll make it." He adjusted his books under his arm. "I hope you do."

"Well thanks." I'd never imagined it would mean any difference to Fletcher Larkin, how we made out.

"Any time you want to use the study hall," Fletch edged past my bike, "just make yourself at home." He started up the lawn to the school while I had to ride around by the gravel road. I couldn't help thinking that even if I didn't have any friends left in Crestview by now, Fletcher Larkin was as nice a guy as I'd ever been on the outs with.

And from then on it got to be less and less friendly. I didn't look forward to eleven o'clock anymore. That's the time those papers got passed around, where you signed up for the ball game after lunch. I was getting to be one of the last ones it got passed to. That morning, even though we were playing touch football these days which has eleven to a side instead of nine, no paper came my way at all. I went home for lunch.

Two days after, I found the X15 was in Istanbul. I heard it from a couple of kids at the coke machine who were arguing whether Istanbul was in Egypt or Turkey. It's in Turkey. And it's about fifteen hundred miles past Bagdad which we hadn't even reached yet when I got off. The outright fact had to be that the X15 had never stopped rolling for even one day to make all that mileage through Arabia and across the deserts and into Turkey without me.

I went looking for one of the X15 and met Pete Feddersen under the covered walk outside. "How about it?" I stopped and stared, to give him a chance to speak up whether I was a half-fledged or a no-fledged any member of the X15 at all. He yelled "Mike!" at some guy behind me and just kept going. Which was as good an answer, I guess, as any.

That afternoon, a stream of third graders tagged on to me as I was cutting across the patio, all of them fit to bust. "Who's Henry Three?" some of them yelled.

The others answered, "He's our Hero!"

"Where does he live?" yelled the first bunch.

"In a Super Zero!"

They kept yelling it over and over for as long as I could hear them, pedaling fast as I could to get away from school.

Our house was in a shambles. It was the new furniture we ordered when Dad made Vice-President. Through some second cousin, Ma worked a miracle to get delivery so fast and now a whole truck load of the stuff showed up.

Ma and Sis were happier than I'd seen them in days, their arms stuffed with wrapping paper and excelsior. The two of them kept shoving things around, with Agnes and Lady, studying the effect. It was pretty good looking furniture, if it comes to that, except some of the chairs that were built out of steel and leather. But even these turned out to be a lot more comfortable than you'd expect, once you sat down in them. It took hours, long after Dad came home, to get everything arranged. But once we did and the floor got vacuumed, the house looked great.

"At last," Ma looked around with a happy sigh. "We're all set."

That remark brought an end to the good time we were having. Considering there was nothing left to get set for. Now we had the furniture there was no one around to invite to the house to see how fine it looked.

The phone rang and that startled us. Sis went into a slide but all she said was "No. That's all right," and she hung up. "Wrong number," she explained.

We all nodded at that because it figured, little as we expected anyone to call. Ma asked. "Who were they looking for?"

Sis shrugged. "Some one named Walsh," she said. "An insurance man. I never heard of any Walsh around Crestview."

Mr. Walsh and his insurance, he was in our arithmetic, the homework Fletcher Larkin and I did that one time together. It could be Fletcher who made the call. It was a signal, maybe, that for some reason he wanted to get in touch with me. As long as he might be taking that much of an interest, I thought I might as well look into it. I wandered out to the garage for my bike.

All you could see of The Mansion in the light of the faraway street lamp was the big oak tree, high as a cloud, and the white end of the front veranda. Upstairs one of the windows was lit and downstairs, the library.

He was happy enough when he opened the side door. "I knew you'd get it," he pointed between his eyes, "with all that voltage you pack up there."

"You mean Mr. Walsh? It only seemed logical."

"Logic. That's the deal I've been using. I've been thinking about you, Henry Three. The fix you're in."

"That's certainly good of you, to go to the trouble."

"I never expected to come up with anything, the head I carry around. But I was taking a shower and a thought came up. Just the thing you need. I couldn't wait to tell you. That's why I called. You don't mind, do you?"

"When you're out to help a guy? I'm thankful to you. Especially if you got some idea how to stop wars."

"Maybe not that. But it's just as good." Fletch shook his fist at me. "If all you want is to get rid of that shelter."

"How?"

"You blow it up!" His hands went into the air like I was out at first. "It's pure simple logic, isn't it?"

"Maybe so," was as far as Fletch would let me answer.

"One five gallon can of gasoline, that's all. You light it up and toss it into the shelter and Carrumph! All you got left is a big hole."

"That won't do."

"Why not? You fill up the hole, you plant some grass and that's the end of it. So you had an accident, that's all. But you're rid of the thing and pretty soon this place forgets you ever had it. And you've back with Pete and Ray and those guys, making it big in Crestview again."

"Nothing doing."

"Why not? That's what you want, isn't it?"

"Yes, I guess it is."

Fletch quieted. "Well, that's what I thought." He let the door swing wide and he leaned against it, in the light that came from the room inside. "Not that I care what you want. I just hate to see anyone like you get squeezed out of here. And if the only thing you need is a five gallon can of gasoline, well!"

"Except the Super Zero, all I've been wanting to tell you, doesn't burn."

"No?"

"And it doesn't Carrumph either. You can't blow the

thing up because the steel can stand all kinds of overpressure. Maybe the insides would get singed. But all'd happen is they'd fix it up again."

"That's all?" Fletch smacked his forehead with the palm of his hand, disgusted with himself. "I guess it only stands to reason. Any idea I thought up, there'd have to be something wrong with it. Birdbrain," he called himself. "Except there did seem a lot of logic to it."

"There's nothing wrong with the idea from that angle," I certainly agreed. "It's full of logic."

"Except I made you chase over here for nothing," said Fletch. "I'm sorry about that."

"It's all right." I told him. "I was looking to get out of the house anyway." I sat down on the side rail of the porch. "On such a nice night. This whole week, the weather's been nice."

Fletch looked around at the weather. "Dry," he said. "They need a good soaking rain through this part of the island."

"I wouldn't know about that, about general conditions."

I waited for anything else Fletch might say. At last he stretched slow and hard. "I guess you got be going, don't you?"

"Not exactly." From the rail I was on, I could see past him to the long table where his books were spread out. "All I have to get back to is homework."

"Say," Fletch laughed. "That's what I'm in the middle of, homework."

"No reason," I mentioned, "that is if you feel like it, we couldn't do it together."

"You mean it?" He made room for me through the

door. "Then come on in." He pulled out a seat under the colored glass lamp and not only laid out pencils and paper but went to the kitchen for drinks, cold milk for him and an orange soda for me.

We went to work on math again, about some used car salesman that had us figuring depreciation and installment payments. Pretty soon Fletch was talking, again, about getting up in class and showing Miss Dokstra. I wasn't going to let anything happen to spoil things, like the last time, so I really bore down on Larkin, working him over with reverse questions until I was absolutely sure he knew what he was doing.

"How about it?" he asked me. "Can I show Dokstra?"

"You're set," I closed the math book. "Only those bases you go around, just remember to touch them all."

"What a bomb that was!" Fletch roared, remembering Mr. Walsh and his insurance. "But this time I'll take it easy, coach," he promised. "And I sure want to thank you for helping me out."

"Any time." I stood up, long as we were finished. "I always told you I'd be glad to come over."

"You mean I can just call you, any time?"

"Well!" The state Ma and Sis were in, that'd be the last straw. If the only calls that came into the house were from the one other family in town nobody spoke to. We fixed it so that Fletcher would telephone the way he did that night, as if it were a wrong number. Only to make sure we didn't get fouled up with someone actually calling a wrong number, I suggested Fletch ask for names according to the alphabet; Mr. Allen, Baker, Cook and so on, so I'd recognize the call was from him.

"That'll do it," Fletch led the way to the door. It was still black on the little porch, with no moon, and there was nothing to see ahead. "But look, Henry Three, there's no question you have to come. I mean no one's forcing you, the way it was."

"You don't have to tell me." I felt my way down the walk to the picket fence. "You can't force me to do anything, Larkin, not anymore. What can you say about me now that would make things worse?"

"That's right, isn't it?" Fletch closed the door and I heard him sit down on the one step of the porch. "So the only reason you'd come over is because you felt like it?"

"I guess so. Just about."

"You don't say!" Fletch must've found a stick. I heard him break it up, two sharp cracks. "Except you're not going to get much chance to come over here, Henry Three, or do anything else in Crestview, unless you think fast. You don't have a lot of time."

"Why not?" We were only a couple of voices talking in the dark.

"Because this place, once it gets down on you, they're fiends. I'm not talking just about ourselves. There was the Lemkes last year, a family lived over on Magnolia Drive. I never knew what started it but they got ripped to pieces, the Lemkes. They were out of here in three months."

"I don't think that'll happen to us."

"Of course not," said Fletch. "Once you get your idea how to stop wars."

Somewhere in the night there was a cricket left over from the summer, kind of weak and occasional. And the big oak tree up top found a wind you didn't feel below and thrashed some. Those were the only sounds.

"I'm not much help but I'm willing to keep trying with you," said Fletch, "as far as thinking goes. For instance, tomorrow afternoon. Case you're not doing anything."

"My plans," I mentioned, "are nothing urgent."

"I've got a pretty good kite we can fly. Over to Bayside Meadows. You know Louie who works for us, he'd drive us out."

"Well sure. That sounds good."

"At least," said Fletch. "It'll give us something to do while we're thinking."

For a little while we listened to that cricket, feeble as it was. The tree high up finished and stood quiet overhead. There wasn't any breeze left, only a sigh in the distance that thinned out and got lost. I opened the gate and felt for my bike. "Take it easy," I said.

"I'll be seeing you." Fletch came down and pulled the gate back on its latch. "Not to say hello or anything like that when we're at school. So that's no problem. I'll just be seeing you."

But even that way, it was a real satisfaction. To be in touch, at least with someone else.

So when a thing happened like Arnie Untermeyer backing away from the blackboard to end up sitting on Miss Dokstra's lap, you could look back to Fletch to see how he was taking it. Instead of laughing by yourself in the middle of twenty-five laughing kids. And when Fletch knocked off the arithmetic next day, handling the whole automobile deal just right, perfect, he walked back to his seat polishing one finger nail on his chest. He didn't have to look my way for us both to be satisfied about it, together.

After school I waited out on the North Shore Turnpike for Larkin's big black Dusenberg to show up. It had to be forty years old at least, their limousine, and it was all corners except for the mudguards that swooped like wings over the wheels. It came along bright and shiny as the day it was delivered. Inside it was overstuffed in blue with heavy curtains curving back and even cutglass vases hanging near the door with flowers in them, small asters, the blue kind. I sat up front with Fletch and Louie because the back was filled with the biggest kite I ever came across, six feet high and red.

He certainly knew what to do with a kite, Fletch did. Once Louie left us, after running around and forever touching one finger to the black peak of his hat, it wasn't ten minutes before he had the thing riding high into the sky far up.

Of course, the Meadows themselves were a prime help. You wouldn't want a better place for flying, this slow rise of land covered with Queen Anne's lace that built up out of the swamp below. We had a lifting wind that came off the Sound with a smell to it that was rusty and sweet, like rotted wood, but clean to breathe and fresh.

Larkin had a reel he'd made with Louie's help, the size of a regulation football with a brake attachment on a little wooden stand, and the low hum came out of it tuned higher and higher until the kite overhead looked no larger than normal. Once it was up, even though I'd never had much to do with a kite before, Fletch made me take over and it felt strange, almost like handling something alive, the way that bit of red showed habits of its own you had to get used to, like the pass to the left it made when you tightened too hard. It could've been a fish on the line except you were the one who was down at the bottom of the clear pond that the sunny afternoon had turned into. And once you did get the kite answering each move you made, it got to feel you were up there with it, yourself, a part of the clouds that went by and the wind.

Fletch tested for different currents of air and picked up a steady blow out of the southeast, way up on the ceiling, that gave him a chance to put the kite into what was almost a dance, stalling and turning and flipping up into a slow half loop. It was nothing to what a kite would do in the hands of a real pro, Fletch described, the ones you'd find in Indo-China and through there. He talked of professional kite flyers, something I'd never heard of, who met in tournaments big as our world series to fly kites with blades attached where the winner was the one who'd cut the strings of all the others. From his grandfather Fletch knew as much about the history of kites, almost, as he did about flying them.

"How did you ever get started, you know, with kites."

"Klein," said Fletch.

"Gardner put you up to it?"

"Back when he moved into Crestview. Gardner told me to go fly a kite. So I asked myself, why not? And when I tried it, I liked it." Fletch wound the reel in a couple of feet. "Besides for anyone by himself where could you find a better sport?"

"Except it's got to get lonely, all the time flying kites."

Fletch explained there was plenty else for him to do, with his Grandfather and helping Louie with projects around The Mansion. Besides over at Bayside there were families the Larkins knew from a way back who had plenty of kids to run with over week ends. "Anyway," he asked me, "what's lonely?"

"Just no one around to talk to."

"Well if that's it, to listen to the Old Man, my Grandpa, there's a lot of people who put in a good deal of time together with no one to talk to. About anything they really want to say, that is." The cord tightened and Fletch let the kite climb. "The Old Man thinks lonely is something you're going to come up against anyway. So you might as well get into condition for it."

"I never heard it was anything you can train for."

"Maybe not. But, for instance, it helps if you belong to something."

"I guess it would. Do you?"

"Sure. To what's around here. This country was practically all Larkin."

"Well, as far as that goes. But I thought you meant belong to an outfit of some kind, with people in it."

"Fact is, I do."

"You belong to a club with other guys."

"There's plenty of others. A lot of them happen to be dead. But that's only because it's old."

"The club is?" I watched him reel in again. "What's the name of it?"

"It's sort of a secret."

"A secret society? With passwords and handshakes?"

"Some of those, yes."

That turned things around. If there was anyone in Crestview more by himself than I was, I thought it'd be Fletcher Larkin. Now it comes out he belonged to a whole organization no one ever heard of. Plus, it looked like Fletch was going to keep right on not letting anyone hear about it. He went to working the kite as if he wanted to skip the whole subject. I didn't think there was anything, now that Fletch and I were talking, we couldn't talk about.

"Like the ones who belong," I asked him, "couldn't you mention some of their names?"

"I can tell you three who don't belong," Fletch braked the reel and looked up at me. "Ray Sattersley, Pete Feddersen and Gardner Klein."

I got the message. As long as those were the ones I wanted to stay in Crestview for, I didn't have any right to go asking Fletch for any of his secrets. I guess that was only fair. It was a letdown, though, far as I was concerned.

"How about pulling it in?" I looked up at the kite. "So we can get out of here."

"Weren't we going to put in time thinking?"

"What's the use? I'm never coming up with any idea how to stop wars."

Fletch stared at me. "What are you giving up for?"

"I've been thinking about it for three whole days."

"Well sure, I know. The trouble is," Fletch hauled in some slack, "you ought to have somebody to think with who's a lot less stupid than I am." He whipped the cord and in a little while, like an echo you looked at, the kite slid away and rounded into a dive that ended with a slow climb back to where it started. "You know who?" Fletch let the kite sail away on its own, pulling the reel. "The Old Man. There's nothing he doesn't know about. He's the one to set you straight, Henry. My Grandfather."

126

12

THERE WERE VERY FEW IN CRESTVIEW WHO HAD EVER seen Mr. Larkin. And no one I heard of ever talked with him. But I thought I might as well take a chance, seeing as how I didn't have much chance left to get the idea I needed.

It was all handled very formal, the meeting was. A regular appointment was set up for four-thirty the next day. I had to wear a jacket, Fletch advised, as well as a necktie. So I showed up at The Mansion looking like I was getting graduated. Louie had us wait for a little while in the big hall downstairs before we could go see Mr. Larkin. But he was hard to see when we went up and first stepped into his room.

It was me who was getting stared at. By a whole collection of men and women in different sizes and shapes, every one of them dressed historical. The big ones hung on the wall, oil paintings they'd have to be, in heavy gold frames that had their own little light overhead. The other pictures were all over the place, crowding the tables and the bookshelves and the mantel of the fireplace where a small flame gave the room an autumn smell, leaves burning.

He came to life behind the crowded desk that stood in the bay window where, outside, hung the big oak tree. He was a tall man and bald except for a horseshoe fringe of gray hair, with lots of eyebrows. The long hands he had were always working and he wore a kind of a jacket I never saw before, reddish brown with a belt. And the smile he had, Mr. Larkin, was like there was a secret that he and I shared together.

"You're Fletcher's friend," he took my hand. "Henry Three."

"It's not so much we're friends," Fletch explained. "We just see each other."

"Well, whatever." Mr. Larkin noticed me looking at all the pictures. "If you're interested you can meet them." He described the most important ones, those in the heavy frames, with dates that went back past 1776 which is the year I always think American history started. "They're all from hereabouts," Mr. Larkin mentioned as if you might run across them shopping any afternoon down at The Marketplace.

He sat me in a big leather chair facing one corner of the desk and helped himself to a cigar out of a shined up wooden box that had a running deer carved into it. Holding the lid, he offered me the box.

"Have one," he said.

"A cigar?"

"Only if your taste runs that way."

It was divided, the case was, on one side cigars and on the other long twisted sticks of licorice. I took one of those and so did Fletch and we chewed while Mr. Larkin made his way, carefully working over his cigar, clipping it and rolling it and heating the end with a match and lighting it, back around the desk to his seat.

"Well now," he faced us, "to what do we owe the pleasure of this visit, Henry Three?"

"He wanted to ask you how to stop wars," said Fletch.

"Ah yes." Mr. Larkin nodded as if it were an ordinary kind of question that might come from anyone you happened to meet. He thought about it, operating his cigar until he had it drawing real smooth. "That's a fairly simple proposition."

"What's that?" I wasn't sure I'd heard him.

"You really mean it?" asked Fletch.

"There's no problem about stopping wars, thank Heavens. Just a little more silence, a stop for good to any talk about the pride and glory we get out of them, and you'll see. They'll be gone for good."

"Wars?"

"Of course, Henry. You never hear of anyone declaring a war nowadays, do you? We're about finished with that kind of surgical nonsense."

"But isn't there, Mr. Larkin, I mean there's still a good deal of fighting goes on."

"To be sure. For a vastly different reason, though. Everyone's defending himself. That's the latest idea for starting a fight. Defense. You take any big self-respecting

130

country, whether it's us or Russia or China or France, there's nowhere in the world they won't go to defend themselves. It's a shift in the way we look at things. We hate war. But we can't blame a man for defending himself, can we?"

"No, sir," said Fletch.

"That's what the fighting's about, all our armies and navies. Defense."

"But isn't that just as bad, sir? I mean," I asked Mr. Larkin, "when you get right down to it?"

"Just as bad. It's much worse, so help me. A lot worse."

"How can you say that?" asked Fletch.

Mr. Larkin took a look at the end of his cigar. "Well, with wars, Fletcher, down through the years there was only one final goal to fighting a war. You wanted to win it. That's all. It was a simple, uncomplicated idea. You marched out to prove you were a better man than the one on the other side. And naturally you'd just as soon see him alive at the end, the other fellow, so he could admit he was beaten."

"That follows." I said.

"Until by the end of the seventeenth century, in through there, wars had more rules than a basketball game. You maneuvered and you campaigned and you besieged and when you did have a battle you managed to kill a lot less people then we do on a Sunday afternoon in traffic. But now," Mr. Larkin swiveled in his chair toward the side window, "with everyone defending themselves, the big aim is to annihilate the other side. The best defense, after all, is to be the only one left."

"No question about that," said Fletch.

"That's why it's so much worse," Mr. Larkin pointed out.

"But look, sir." I swallowed the last of my licorice. "How about that? If no one wants to fight wars, it ought to be simple to get everyone to quit defending themselves against each other."

"That's not who they're defending themselves against, Henry Three. Not each other."

"Then from who?"

"That's not the question either. It's from what?"

"I'm sorry sir. From what?"

"Machinery. The only big secrets that frighten us anymore, they're not human, Henry, they're machine-made. They keep rolling out at us, all those new machines, until there seems no way left to stop them from coming. So we try to defend ourselves, against the newest submarine, the newest airplane, the newest high-priority bomb. We keep looking for protection against the next invention coming up. That's what scares us. Tomorrow's top-secret machine."

We watched, Fletch and I, while Mr. Larkin carefully carried the ash of his cigar to a clean tray on his desk where he rolled it off, intact. "Does that clear it up for you?" he asked me.

"Not so much," I had to admit. "Near as I can understand, you think we ought to stop inventing machines."

"We can't, Henry Three. What I'm saying is, we don't know how to stop. What has stopped, let's face it, is much more important. We've stopped inventing a new kind of man. That's a job we used to be magnificent at. Since the beginning of time we kept turning ourselves out better and better. It's hard to believe, the inventing that brought us from a floating blob in the ocean to an upright man. That's stopped. And there's your problem, Henry Three. You've got to get us back to inventing a better kind of human being again." He waited, watching from under his big eyebrows.

"Who? Me?" I squared off the cigar box on his desk. "There's no chance for anything like that."

"Why not? You're young enough," he smiled, "to do a lot of experimenting. And you seem to be taking this seriously enough, this whole question." He waved his smoke away. "I was wondering, why?"

"Because Henry Three's going to have to leave Crestview, that's all," said Fleach. "Less he finds a way to stop wars."

"So that's it. Crestview. Well!" Mr. Larkin noticed the fire and pulled out of his chair to cross the room so he could shift a log. "To my mind, you understand, that's no great tragedy. Having to leave Crestview. Especially for you, Henry Three, pleased as I am to meet you. This is no place for a boy to grow up to be a man."

"Why not, sir?"

"There are no men here." A blaze started up in the fireplace and Mr. Larkin put away his poker. "On this fine October afternoon, I warrant I'm the only full grown man in Crestview who's not delivering something."

"Well of course, if that's what you're getting at. No fathers show up until the 5:43."

"That's exactly what I'm getting at, Henry Three. You're living in a woman's world here. Crestview is her idea."

"Just because there are no men around during the day?"

"That's the simple fact. But the reasons go deep. Crestview is built on two ideas. They're the only two ideas the women around here really believe, far as I can see. One of them is what we've just been talking about. Defense."

"I don't see where they're so interested in that," said Fletch. "In the army and navy."

"Then let's call it protection. Or better yet, security. They're all the same thing. It's simply that these women have to be safe. They have their children to protect. Their first big idea is to get enough security to bring up a family. And the second, they have to be in fashion. Because in a place like this a woman can't grow old. Every year she has to look new again, as if she's just starting out. Well now," Mr. Larkin tried a puff at his cigar which was dead. He looked around the mantel and found a box of matches. "I don't say there's anything wrong with those two ideas, style and security. But so help me, they're not big enough, that's all. Not for Crestview. And not for the world that's managed by all the Crestviews that have grown up around us."

He cleaned the end off his cigar, tipping it into the fireplace with his little finger, and he lit up again.

"You've got the wrong idea, Grandpa." Fletch finally spoke up. "You're trying to tell Henry Three he ought to get out of here. That's not what he wants. He wants to stay here. He likes it here."

"Whatever for?" Mr. Larkin got his cigar back into business, puffing away. "You're a discerning young man, Henry. What do you find so attractive about living in a place like this, a suburb?"

"I don't know, sir. There are things about it," I explained. "One thing, it's the latest. It's modern."

"Perhaps the plumbing is." Mr. Larkin shook his head. "Not the ideas we've been talking about, the ideas it lives by. They're about thirty-five hundred years old. That's how far back you'd have to go to find a world anything like Crestview, a matriarchy."

I looked to Fletch and he shrugged.

"Matriarchy. A society that's ruled by women. Ma, the name you call your mother, she started out as a Hittite goddess back in Asia just about the time we began to write history. And there you have it, why Crestview's wrong." Mr. Larkin made it back to his chair behind the desk. "We can't go reaching back thirty-five hundred years, not with all those inventions coming up tomorrow. Fashion's fine and so is security, but they're not enough to control a lot of machinery. If we can't find anything better to live by than those two things, we might as well give this particular planet back to the ants."

He swiveled around to look at the oak tree. And for a while there was nothing left to think about except maybe the ants Mr. Larkin mentioned. Fletch leaned across to where I sat. "I'm sorry," he whispered.

His Grandfather didn't turn. "What are you sorry about, Fletcher?"

"Nothing, sir. Except I just about guaranteed Henry Three you'd tell him what he wanted, so he could stay in Crestview."

Mr. Larkin kept studying out the window. "I tried to do a great deal better than that, Fletcher. I've given your friend good reason never to be sorry to leave here."

"He's not my friend," Fletch reminded his grandfather. "It's just we see each other."

"When it comes to that," Mr. Larkin glanced around, "you two are splitting a pretty fine hair, aren't you?"

"Not really," said Fletch.

"It just happened to work out that way," I told Mr.

Larkin.

"Well, if you can manage a relationship that intricate, I don't think you really need any help from me. If I've been any help." Mr. Larkin went back to inspecting the oak tree outside. "About the best you can do at my age is to excuse yourself for the world you pass along. That's all I've been doing, maybe, just offering you an apology. You needn't accept it." He leaned forward to look out of the side of the window. "As a matter of strict fact, there's only one thing I've come to be absolutely positive about."

"What's that, sir?" I asked him.

"The wind's out of the southeast. It's going to rain."

"That's for sure," said Fletch.

"And while I have considerable faith in you two, that you'll grow into men who can measure up to any machine that's ever patented, do you know what my immediate hope is?"

"No, sir." I said.

"It's for that tree. The leaves are starting to turn. And the oak's a miracle when it comes into color. I only hope the storm doesn't strip it bare."

"I hope so too," I told him.

"Why," Mr. Larkin swung around to look at me from under his eyebrows. "That's extremely kind of you, Henry Three."

"It's just I want to thank you," I said.

"Whatever for?" He let me have that smile again, as if we had a secret together. "The licorice?" He winked at the cigar box. "Have some more."

13

"YOU DON'T WANT TO TAKE THAT PERSONAL," SAID Fletch. "Where Grandfather suggested you ought to leave Crestview. It's only a general notion he has."

"Even so. He was just about our last chance. Far as I see, we're finished."

We were out in the front yard under the big tree that had been standing there for the last three hundred years. It was braced with guy wires thick as lead pipes, and heavy turnbuckles that were rusted solid. We leaned against the wires and finished our licorice.

"We'll get an idea, don't you worry," promised Fletch, "if we just keep trying."

"I don't expect so, not anymore. All that's left is to thank you, Fletch. I sure appreciate you trying so hard to help me. Especially, with everything else you have to do."

"Me? Like what?"

"With that secret society you belong to."

"Oh that," said Fletch. "Think nothing of it. Hardly takes up any time at all. The thing is, Henry, you can't let yourself get discouraged."

"Why not? What difference would it make anyway, even if our family does have to leave Crestview? I mean to you, tied up as you are?"

"Who's tied up?"

"With that secret society we just mentioned."

"Look!" Fletch took a kick at the guy wire. "That secret society you're always bringing up, maybe I ought to explain that I'm the only member that's active."

"I thought you said there was a crowd that belonged to it."

"Sure, there's hundreds. There's Grandpa. Except the cellar where we hold our meetings got too damp for him. And all the other members, the trouble is they died centuries ago. The thing began in 1491."

"Before Columbus?"

It was real enough, Fletcher's secret society. It was called the True Brotherhood of the Outer Reaches. The name came from Holland where points of land that stick out into the ocean are called *reaches*. The True Brotherhood had a castle on one of them that was built by a couple of long ago uncles of the Larkins, who helped to get the society started.

That's how Grandpa Larkin happened to know about it, through a book that got passed down in the family. And after Fletcher's father and mother died, Mr. Larkin thought it might be a good idea for the two who were left to join up. So they initiated each other. Fletch and his Grandfather. Fletch remembered the meetings they held down in the cellar, with candles and feasts, as one of the best things that happened to him when he was a kid. Nothing like that though went on anymore because Mr. Larkin's arthritis didn't give him much chance to sit around in a cellar.

"So it doesn't take up so much of my time," Fletch described. "After all an organization with only one member can't have too many activities."

"I can see that," I had to agree.

"It's the honor mostly," said Fletch. "When you read about some of the members, how they went around settling other people's arguments, the things they did, it's not the activities that are so important. It's an honor, the biggest one I ever ran into, just to belong to the True Brotherhood of the Outer Reaches."

"I guess you're lucky." And it certainly changed what I had in mind, the picture of Fletch running around swapping passwords and handshakes with a bunch of his own guys. It made us even again. The two of us were both on our own, together.

"As far as luck goes," Fletch swung around the guy wire to face me, "in case you're interested, the True Brotherhood is always looking for new members."

"If you mean me, sure, I'm interested. How does it happen?"

"I can always get Grandpa down for another meeting. And then if there's a majority vote that someone qualifies, he gets initiated."

"How do you get to qualify?"

"To begin with, you have to live around here."

"That sounds simple enough."

Fletch shook his head. "Not for you it doesn't." He shinnied up the heavy rusted cable. "You tell me you're finished here in Crestview." He looked down at me. "That there's no use thinking any more. As far as I can see, you've quit and you're ready to leave."

"If that's what you're getting at." I picked at some of the splintered wire in front of me. "One thing, now I know about the True Brotherhood, that makes a difference."

"Enough so you want to keep trying?"

"I wouldn't mind."

Fletch dropped to where I was. "That's the way I like to hear you talk, Henry. And I tell you if you do manage to stay on here, it's practically certain I can get you into the Brotherhood. I can almost promise. And when you consider that'll just about double the active membership, there'll be twice as many activities. It's liable to be great."

"Then maybe we ought to start thinking again."

"How to stop wars? Let's go, Henry. I'm right with you." Fletch banged the wire. "How do we get started?"

"You keep quiet and you're started."

I sat against the tree and Fletch hung from one of the wires and we stared at each other. In the minutes that went by nothing came to my mind. And the look in Fletcher's eyes started to get glazed. It got to be uncomfortable, just staring. I picked at the bark of the tree. Fletch found some leaves and carefully ripped them to shreds.

After a while he said, "There has to be a better way than this."

"None I ever heard of."

"Isn't there some way to handle it, for instance, like doing arithmetic. It'd be easier if it was the same as Mr. Walsh, you remember, and his insurance."

"Well, this has nothing to do with insurance. Except," I reminded myself, "the President of A. L. & L. he talked about insurance. Mr. Matthews said bomb shelters were like insurance."

"Where's the connection? Insurance is only if a man dies or gets killed then he gets paid what his policy is worth. That's all it is."

The way Fletch put it brought up a thought somehow. "With insurance," I went over it again word for word, "if a man gets killed he has to get paid."

"That's what I just said."

"So if you sold a man insurance," slowly I bent the piece of bark in my hand and it broke, "you'd want to keep him alive, wouldn't you?"

"Of course, what are you getting at?"

"I don't know." There was something revolving though, like a picture coming on to a T.V. set, all out of focus and in a whirl. Then it cleared. I saw it sharp. "It's a western," I pointed at Fletch. "You and me. We're looking to kill each other. Now listen! I come out of the saloon. You come out of the hotel. We reach and we're ready to draw. But we don't. We stand there, stiff."

"Why? How come?"

"Because you're the one sold me an insurance policy. For maybe a hundred thousand dollars. So what'd happen if you killed me?"

"I'd have to pay you a hundred thousand dollars."

"Same with me. I sold you a policy too. And if I killed you, I'd be the one who'd have to pay out a hundred thousand dollars. Would I kill you?"

"I guess not," said Fletch "Not at those prices."

"That's why those two are standing there. They can't kill each other. It's too expensive."

"No, maybe not. But it couldn't ever happen. Cowboys don't sell insurance."

"I'm not thinking of cowboys."

"What are you thinking?"

"I don't know yet. But there's something coming, Fletch. Something." I rolled over on my stomach and started to rip grass. There did look to be something just out of reach, practically at the end of my fingertips. And slowly as I could, I tried closing in on it. Then even before it came along, I felt a lightness growing up inside of me as if I knew the idea already and was only trying to remember it, just bring it to mind. I took the grass out of my hand, one blade at a time, and carefully built it up into a pile. It came sweet as the smell of fresh earth, the whole idea. I had it.

"Fletch," I whispered. "I think I know how."

"To stop wars?"

"Yes."

"How?"

"Give me another couple of seconds, Fletch. That's all."

He sat there, leaning against the tree trunk and he didn't move. He watched me, whatever I did, and he waited. Most of the time I lay in the grass looking up through the leaves of the big oak at the high patches of blue that were clouding up for the rain, I guess, Mr. Larkin mentioned. I went over the idea time after time until it locked tight. Then I sat up.

"Okay Fletch. Here it is. Instead of those cowboys."

"Yes."

"Imagine it's the United States and Russia."

"Right."

"Just suppose that every last insurance policy in the United States was sold here by Russia. And just suppose every last life insurance policy in the U.S.S.R. was sold over there by the U.S.

"I see."

"Then the Russians, they're not going to let go with any bombs to kill millions of people they got insured. Not when they have to pay off all those policies. And that goes for us, too. No country's going to kill you that's staking so much money you keep alive. They can't. They'd ruin themselves."

Fletch nodded. "One second," he said. "Let's see if I understand." He counted it off on his fingers. "Russia, they got all us insured. And us, we got all their lives insured. Then if they kill off fifty million Americans at a hundred thousand dollars apiece, or even twenty thousand dollars! Screaming Jehoshaphat, there's not that much money in the world." Fletch looked at me wide-eyed.

"Maybe not."

"All she'd have to hit us with is a couple of good hydrogen bombs," Fletch went on breathless, "and Russia, she'd be out of business right then and there. And vice versa Hank, if we hit them, we'd be bankrupt. The way you're talking, you couldn't have a war. If you ever won it, you'd be ruined. It'd wreck you for good. You see what I mean?"

"I see what you mean."

"All I'm saying is no country could afford to go to war on that basis. Even if they lost, they'd be done for. This whole idea just about makes wars impossible, if you follow me?"

"I follow you."

Fletch stopped short. "What do you mean, you follow me? It's your idea."

"It sounds just as good the way you put it."

"But one second." He quieted and gave me a worried look. "Why should the Russians come over here to buy their life insurance?"

"That'd take a law," I told him. "Just one international law, where no one can buy their life insurance in any country that's friendly. Like us here, we have to go to Russia to get a policy, or to China or Cuba or any other country that hates us. Just as soon as a country starts hating us, it has to take on a share of insuring our lives."

"And we theirs."

"Naturally. The U.S. has to sell insurance to anybody we don't agree with."

"I get you." Fletch came to his feet. "It's a simple enough law. And every country would have to pass it."

"Same as every country has laws against murder and robbery," I said. "Because if they didn't, any country like that, no one for certain would insure their lives. They'd be dead ducks."

"Dead ducks." Fletch offered me his hand and pulled

me to my feet. "All I want to say, Henry." But he had nothing to say. Instead he was gone, racing around the front of the house. I chased after to see what was up. Fletch let out one screaming steam whistle of a yell heading down the side around some hydrangea bushes. He cut across the back through a vegetable garden. He curved around to the front yard past the little porch of the library. When he reached the oak tree again he took off for one of the guy wires, catching it high and climbing. He swung for the cable beyond and he missed. He landed in a heap.

"Henry Three you've got it." With no breath left, Fletch was hoarse. "It all checks out. It works."

"Far as I can see," I panted.

"I knew you'd get the idea you needed. Now it's here."

"I think so."

"You're in Crestview for good."

"Well." I tried to explain how first I had to tell my father. And how he'd have to write up a report about the idea. And then how Mr. Matthews would have to read it and give his okay before A. L. & L. would go out of the shelter business and take back the Super Zero. Fletch wasn't too interested in the details, now we knew how to stop wars. "Henry Three," he kept saying, "you're a marvel. You're going to go down in history. There's practically a thousand I.Q. in that one idea alone."

So it was rough, what I had to tell Fletcher Larkin, about the complications I ran into with the family. I knew he was waiting at The Mansion that night for some word how my father liked the idea. But there was nothing to report. And it was no night for bike riding. Just as Mr. Larkin expected, it began to rain.

All the calls that came into the house, for Mr. Allen and Mr. Baker and Mr. Cook got in the way of my father who was working at the dining room table. After someone asked to speak with Mr. Davis and Mr. Earl, Dad called the telephone company to complain about all the wrong numbers we were getting. The last call was for Mr. Phillips. I could see how anxious Fletch was getting if the best *F* he could think up was Phillips.

Even at school next day there was no chance to describe to Fletch what happened. On account of the rain that kept up, everywhere indoors was crowded with no chance to get together by ourselves. After the last bell, we both headed for the bus stop but there were people under the shed waiting for an extra heavy burst to pass over. Fletch set off in his yellow slicker and I followed until we ended up in a culvert under the highway. It was dry under the long cement arch but loud, with the noise of the traffic booming overhead, and all spread around with empty beer cans and what was left of tires.

"What's wrong?" Fletch grabbed my bike as I came in. "Don't tell me your father didn't like the idea."

"I never got a chance to tell him."

"For heaven sakes, why not?"

"My mother didn't think I ought to bring it up right now."

"How come? Didn't she like it?"

"She thought it was a fine idea. It's only that Dad hasn't been Vice-President for even a month yet. And Ma didn't feel this was the time for him to be telling Mr. Matthews, you know, how to stop wars. She decided I ought to lay off awhile before I bring it up."

"How long?"

"A couple of months maybe. Something like that."

"Oh no!" Fletch sat down on the frazzled carcass of a big truck tire. "A couple of months," he groaned. "You could be out of here in a couple of months."

"But there's nothing we can do, Fletch."

"Please," Fletch begged me. "Don't talk like that. After the brains you put into it, after the way it shapes up, how it works, we just can't keep an idea like this to ourselves. That'd be terrible! That'd be like Lincoln tearing up the Gettysburg Address without mentioning it to anybody. Or Thomas A. Edison dropping the electric bulb into an ash can before someone else ever got to see it. There has to be something, Henry, something we can do about it."

"Like what?" I found a five gallon oil can to sit on.

"I don't know like what," said Fletch. We had the rain to look at and a sweeping screen of water that curved, every time a car passed overhead, across the arch at the end. "Like if you can't get your father to tell this Mr. Matthews, I don't know," Fletch pounded the tire he sat on, "there ought to be some way you could get the idea across to Mr. Matthews yourself."

Lightning cracked. You could see the rip across the sky through the arch of the culvert. A crash of thunder broke into the tunnel like a freight train rolling through.

"Henry," Fletch sat straight on his tire facing me. "Did you hear that?"

"It struck close."

"Not the lightning. Me. What I thought of."

"When?"

"Just now. Where I said you ought to get the idea across

147

to Mr. Matthews yourself. Why not? Just go and tell it to him."

I couldn't help laugh at Fletch. "It's not that simple."

"Why not? You know where his office is. You go in and lay the whole thing out. Explain it direct, from you to him."

"It doesn't work that way, Fletch."

"What doesn't?"

"To go up there, into those offices." I pointed out through the arch where you'd see the buildings of New York if it weren't so gray and slanted with rain. "They're only about the most important offices in the world. They don't let kids go wandering around up there. The least you have to be is grown-up. Don't I know? Up there is where I'm headed myself, once I'm out of college and Dad can fix it. But there's no chance of getting in to see anybody, much less a President, unless you're grown-up at least and got some pull working for you besides."

Fletch shook his head. "The way you go on, it doesn't make any sense. First your Ma talks about months. You're talking about years! But the trouble you're in is right now." Fletch picked up a beer can and leveled it at me. "If you have to be grown-up to see this Mr. Matthews then I figure, Henry, you've got no time to lose. You'd just better grow up. Not this afternoon maybe. It's too late for that. But tomorrow morning, first thing, you'd better get started."

"To grow up?"

"To get into the city and see Mr. Matthews and let him have the idea you got. And I tell you what. I'll go in with you. We'll skip school and I'll get you in to see Mr. Matthews if I have to kick somebody's door down. We'll do it together."

"We can't, Fletch. Thanks. But it's no use."

Fletch tossed the beer can end over end. He caught it and took to reading the label. Overhead the cars sounded like the break of a wave as they went by. Still studying the beer can, Fletch asked me, "Why do you think, Henry Three, I'm so anxious for you to stay in Crestview?"

"I don't know."

"It's just that you're about the greatest guy who ever showed up here. What do you want to hide it for?"

"Hide what?"

"How good you are. The brains you got. And another thing, you're the only guy here who ever beat me in a fight."

"That was lucky."

"Not altogether. You're fast. And you're tough. Yet you let these guys walk all over you. It's about time you stood up for who you really are. You could practically change the world, the idea you thought up. Don't you even want to try?"

Fletch lobbed the beer can over to me and I had to reach to catch it. When I looked back he was up on his feet with that smile of his, waiting to hear what I had to say. And there's nothing to say to a guy who thinks you're all that good except what he wants to hear. So I told Fletch, "Okay, we'll go in and talk to Mr. Matthews, the President of American Lock and Locomotive."

There was nothing to lose, I thought, except a little school.

14

WE STOOD ON THE DRENCHED SIDEWALK OF 33RD STREET in New York City and we looked up, Fletch and I to the top of where the Empire State Building ought to be. Except there wasn't any top. After thirty or forty stories the building went out of sight, hid in the soft rainy gray that piled high into a mist where you could see the lights of the offices, and then up into a cloud where everything ended, blank and dead.

The storm was worse than ever. Over the air at breakfast, they mentioned the turbulence was on account of some hurricane far out to sea that we were only getting the edge of. The 9:47 into New York was practically empty. It was too late for any of the men commuting, which is why we picked it, and there weren't any women going in to shop, not on such a day.

We made a run for the Empire State Building but the door we hit was a freight entrance, deliveries only. There was an elderly gent there, about the happiest man we saw all morning, who explained we had to head around the corner to the main lobby. He was dumping bags of paper into a big press that clamped the stuff down into squared off bales. "This is what it all comes down to," he hit a switch that dropped the top of the machine with a thud. "Waste paper. Those offices upstairs turn out three or four tons a day."

One whole wall of the main lobby, which smelled cold from the marble and wet from the umbrellas, was a Directory. It listed the names of the companies in the building and American Lock and Locomotive had three whole floors starting with 78. There was nothing left but to go up.

"Why're you so worried?" Fletch asked me.

"I don't know." It wasn't as if anything bad could come out of the trip, or good either. I was only going through the motions of trying to see the President of A. L. & L., after all, to show Fletch that it was impossible. Still, this was the first time I'd ever been to a Home Office. And besides, everyone else looked worried. As if each of them were rushing to keep an appointment where all they could hear was bad news. It was catching.

"Nothing to worry about," said Fletch. We took off our slickers and checked each other, our ties and jackets. The elevator door closed on me and Fletch and three men and a lady, all of us taking care not to look at each other. It was as if it were a minute of silence we were standing for someone who'd passed away while an organ far off played a single note that went up and up until the door opened at the 78th floor.

American Lock and Locomotive was quiet. It was almost white without shadows and soft, the carpets you sank into. There were a good many people around waiting. They sat in big armchairs and heavy couches with their briefcases spread out on coffee tables. No one talked, worried as most of them looked.

In the long quiet room, there was only one decoration, an oversized painting of four lines, two yellow ones and two red. It was a pretty good painting, I guess, if you liked lines. In front of it sat a girl at a fifteen foot desk who was as beautiful as any advertisement. Most of what she said was "Sorry." "Sorry he's out of town," she told the men ahead of us, or, "Sorry he's in a meeting." And then it was our turn.

"Name please?" The beautiful girl looked up from the little pad she wrote on. Since this was as far as we were going to get, anyway, I figured I'd let Fletch handle it.

He said, "Fletcher Larkin." And her pen stopped at the next space on the pad. "Firm?" she wanted to know. "Do you belong to any organization?"

Fletch copied her whisper. "Only the True Brotherhood of the Outer Reaches."

"Brotherhood?" she looked surprised. "A labor union?"

"No ma'm. It's," Fletch waved. "You know."

"Very well. Who'd you want to see?"

"The President."

"Who?"

"Mr. Matthews."

"But surely you don't have an appointment with Mr. Matthews?"

"No ma'm. We just wanted to talk with him for a couple of minutes."

"But that's impossible." She ripped the page off her pad. "I'm sorry," she told Fletch, without going into why she was sorry. It happened just about how I expected. "Name please?" she asked the man behind me. I stepped out of his way. According to my watch, we still had plenty of time to make the 1:10 back to Crestview. Fletch grabbed to keep me from leaving.

"Just a second," he told the girl behind the desk. "We're customers, ma'm. We came here to talk about your Super Zero. And if that's the way you're going to treat someone who's bought one!"

She interrupted. "You should've mentioned that before. Mr. Matthews indeed! If you wish to discuss a product, please write to Consumer Relations." She held out a card.

"Thanks very much," I took it and started off.

Fletch held me. "Write a letter? After we come here in all this rain?"

She smiled at the man waiting beside me. "Very well, I'll try to arrange an appointment," she told Fletch. "If there's someone available in Consumer Relations. Please have a seat."

Fletch pulled me over to a couch. "He's in Room 7820."

"Who?"

"Mr. Matthews. Didn't you see the list of phone numbers she had on her desk? Mr. Matthews was right on top. All we have to do is get to Room 7820."

"But even so," I pointed out to Fletch. Everyone who did have an appointment had to wait until some other girl showed up, all of them out of advertisements, to lead him away. There were only two doors in the long room with no chance of getting through them, on our own. "Besides if we leave now we can get the 1:10 out of Penn Station."

"What's your rush?" said Fletch. "Give me a chance to scout around this place." He meandered past the two doors but just as I expected, they were locked. The receptionist had to push a buzzer with her foot before they opened. Fletch wandered off to the Men's Room for the chance that would give him to find some other doors. My only hope was that it wouldn't take him more than five minutes to get discouraged. That'd still give us time to make our train.

When a thought started circulating, on my own, how actually we could get in to see Mr. Matthews.

To save bucking the weather a lot of people, it looked, were having their lunch sent in. The food showed up in large white boxes carried by kids hardly older than ourselves, all of them practically hidden by their raincoats and hats. And the thing is, not one of them stopped to mess with the beautiful girl at the desk. They flipped past without even a hello and, as she buzzed one of the doors open, they'd head straight for the office the lunch was ordered from.

Why couldn't Fletch and I, the idea developed, do the same thing? And once an idea shows up, you can't help but give it a chance to work. Besides if it did, if we ever did get into Room 7820 and see Mr. Matthews, if it turned out he liked our idea how to stop wars, if he actually did take the Super Zero back, that would be good. What was I thinking? That would be wonderful.

I didn't wait for Fletch. I told the beautiful girl not to

bother any more, we had to leave now, which suited her just as well. I found Fletch wandering past the elevators and pushed him into one that was headed down. It startled him but when he heard what we were up to, he practically took it for granted.

"I was just waiting," he told me, "for you to come up with something. Once you're on a spot, you always do."

We found one of the delivery boys in the lobby downstairs. He told us where some of the lunches were coming from. The Buckingham Coffee Shop across the street.

Heading out of the revolving doors, though, was a surprise. We got blown back. We had to go around again and brace ourselves to shove out on to the sidewalk. The wind was fierce. I didn't see how any of the rain reached the pavement, level as the blast was carrying it straight up Fifth Avenue. It was only by leaning into the force of it so you could almost touch the ground that we made it across the street.

The radio in the Buckingham Coffee Shop went on about nothing but the hurricane over the Atlantic. The announcer described there was a shift that was bringing it closer to New York, close enough so everyone had to take precautions. Already a couple of signs had blown off buildings and someone in the Bronx had a concussion.

We heard it all while they made up the three different lunches we ordered. This was not only to give Mr. Matthews a choice of what to eat in case he turned out to be hungry, we needed enough boxes for carrying to look like the other delivery boys upstairs. Fletch thought we ought to order even more, but we settled on buying a half dozen empty cartons for a quarter which was a saving in money besides cutting down the waste there'd be in pastrami and cole slaw.

In the lobby of the Empire State we made sure that the collars of our slickers were way up and our sou'wester hats pulled down. Upstairs, with Fletch hidden behind four boxes and me carrying five, we headed right past the beautiful girl and made straight for one of the closed doors. I held my breath as we came up to it but, sure enough, it worked. The door buzzed and, juggling the boxes in my arm, I grabbed for the handle. We were through the door, both of us, Fletch and I. We stood right in the middle of American Lock and Locomotive with everywhere we wanted to go just ahead.

"Simple enough," Fletch elbowed me, "Once you know how."

Room 7820 turned out to be a whole collection of offices. In the first there were two men, worried, with their own secretaries, beautiful ones. The next room had wallpaper with hunting scenes and there were two typists under floor lamps. One of them looked up but Fletch said "Lunch" and nodded at the door beyond. They didn't stop us.

The last room was draped in green with the look of a private home and there was only one lady in it. I don't know if you could call her beautiful, the age she was, but she certainly made a fine appearance with her hair all silver and bluish and the pearls she wore.

She was on the phone and she held up her hand to stop us where we were. "I'm sorry for the delay," she said into the phone. "Mr. Matthews is ready to speak with Geneva right now. As soon as you can get Mr. Caldwell."

She hung up. "Go away," she waved at us.

"Lunch," I told her from underneath my hat, "for Mr. Matthews."

"Go away," she hurriedly powdered her nose in a tiny mirror. "You've made a mistake."

Fletch pretended he was reading from the top of a box. "Matthews," he spelled. "Room 7820. This is the right office, isn't it?"

"That's ridiculous." She rushed for a door across from her desk. "Quiet," she shushed us. She opened the door just a crack. "We're through to Switzerland, Mr. Matthews. They're getting him." The phone on her desk rang. "There he is now." She turned back to her desk.

The door swung open. We stood face to face with Mr. Matthews. There he was not fifteen feet away, looking at us.

He was the kind of a man, sitting in a tall leather-backed chair behind a long table with one paper on it and a lamp, where everything about him seemed just enough. He had just enough hair to comb tight to his head. And just enough nose to balance eyeglasses on. There was enough tie to knot and enough handkerchief to show in his coat pocket and the sight of him made you realize that most people carry around a lot of extra curves, shadows and wrinkles on their faces that don't serve any purpose at all. There was nothing missing about Mr. Matthews and there was nothing left over.

He took off his glasses and touched his lips with the end of them, watching us. The lady on the phone said, "I can't accept this connection, the way it crackles. I'll hang on, but please hurry."

It was hard enough getting looked at by Mr. Matthews, much less to say anything. But Fletcher spoke up. "If you're hungry, sir, we got pastrami. Or ham and cheese on rye."

Mr. Matthews shook his head, once. The lady rushed from the telephone to shut the door. "I'm sorry about these young people," she said. But Mr. Matthews closed his eyes slowly. That seemed to tell her it was all right to leave the door open. "I'm holding for a better connection. It's the storm." He closed his eyes again and the lady rushed back to the phone.

He pointed his glasses at us and he actually spoke. "Who are you?"

"Larkin," said Fletch.

"Lovering," I told him.

He nodded and waited to hear what else we had to say.

"It's only Henry here," said Fletch, "he's got an idea for you to stop wars so you can go out of the shelter business. The way it works," Fletcher kicked me. "Go ahead!"

I took a deep breath. "If according to law you could get your life insured by your own worst enemy and he had to sell you as much insurance as you wanted to buy, who'd fight wars?"

A thin gold pencil came into Mr. Matthews' hand. He touched the point of it to the table. "Lovering?" he stared at me.

"Henry Three," said Fletch. "Wait'll you hear how he's got it all worked out."

"Mr. Caldwell," said the lady behind us. "Just fine. As if you were in the next room." She made it to the door again. "It's your call, sir."

But Mr. Matthews had the drawer of his table open and

he wrote inside it with his gold pencil. There was a rip and he held out a small paper. The lady rushed to take it. Mr. Matthews picked up the phone. "Caldwell. I'm sorry I'm late. But I'm afraid," he went on. The lady pulled the door shut.

"Now what is this, you two? Out of here. Scat!" She read the paper.

Fletch groaned. "He never even heard our whole idea."

"He heard enough of it," the lady looked up in surprise, "that he wants something done about it."

"Our idea?" I asked her.

"He likes it?" said Fletch.

"Enough," she pushed the buzzer on her desk, "to give it top priority. Everything stops when one of these comes along."

"How do you like that?" Fletch marveled. "You can see why a guy like that's President. He hears a dozen words and gets the whole idea."

One of the typists came in. "It's an Action Memo, Diana," the lady handed her the paper. "Will you take these boys to 7604."

All the way down those long corridors Fletch and I kept breathing hard at each other. "How he picked it up! In a flash. That's how good it is, Henry. He saw the whole thing clear," said Larkin.

"How could it happen?" I asked him. "How'd we ever do it, Fletch? It worked!"

Diana led the way into another office that was wallpapered with hunting scenes where another secretary, more beautiful right that minute than any of the others, came to her feet at the sight of the memo. "I'm sorry," the secretary took us into an office all paneled in wood. "I'm afraid he won't be here for a minute or two."

I came to a stop staring at myself. It was a picture on the glass-covered desk of me and my mother and Lady and Sis standing in front of a bush.

"Let me out of here," I yelled.

It had to be his office, the one belonged to my Dad.

15

I PILED MY BOXES ON FLETCH AND WENT FOR THE DOOR. The secretary closed it ahead of me. "I got to get out of here," I explained.

"He won't be a minute," she leaned against the shut door. "I'll call him, long as it's an Action Memo from Mr. Matthews."

"Please!" I held the knob. "You don't have to do anything, ma'm. Just let me out of here."

"What gives?" asked Fletch from behind the nine boxes he held.

The knob in my hand turned. I let it go. I stood still. The door opened. He came through, looking at the folder he carried. "Caroline," my father remarked. "If you'd get your book." The sight of me brought him up straight. "Henry Three?" He saw the pile of boxes and the lower

162

half of Fletch. "What is this? What's happening?"

"Hello, Dad," I answered him.

"Mr. Lovering?" Fletcher's voice blasted from behind. "Good morning, sir."

"This just came down from Mr. Matthews," Caroline handed Dad the paper.

"An Action Memo!" Dad looked around at all of us. "About what?"

"Far as I can gather," she said. "It's about them."

"Henry? Henry Three and Mr. Matthews?" Dad's laugh passed quick as a cough. "What's Mr. Matthews got to do with Henry?"

"All I know Mr. Lovering, is Diana," the girl explained. "She brought them down from Mr. Matthews' office."

"But that's impossible," Dad turned to me. "You weren't in Mr. Matthews' office?"

"No, Dad," I told him. "Not all the way in."

"But you saw him? To talk to?"

"Well, you know how he is," I reminded Dad. "He doesn't talk much."

"But you talked?"

"Only a couple of remarks. He was busy with a phone call to Mr. Caldwell. You know, the one in Geneva. So there wasn't all that time, not for conversation."

Dad nodded; he saw what I meant. Then he gave his head a shake, the way you'd clear your ears coming out of a pool. He went to his desk where he put the folder down with the Action Memo on top of it. He dropped into his seat and looked at us. From the expression he had it almost seemed he was trying to laugh, but no sound came out. "How do you like this?" he asked himself.

"You mentioned dictation," said Caroline. "If you want me to bring my book."

He managed to smile at her. "Never mind." She hesitated at the sight of my father, the sudden dry look he had, in case he might need some other kind of help. "Thanks, Caroline. That'll do."

She went through the door with a last glance, at the three of us, that was puzzled.

"If you'll excuse me, sir," came Fletcher's voice. "Is there someplace I can put these down?"

"Just as a start," Dad lifted a finger at the boxes Fletch was holding, "What's that?"

"Lunch is all."

"What's behind it?"

"Only a friend of mine. You know Larkin, don't you? Fletcher Larkin."

"The Larkins? I didn't know Fletcher Larkin was a friend of yours."

"It's not that so much." Fletch looked around the pile in his hands. "It's just we've been seeing each other."

"On the floor will do," Dad suggested to Fletch. "Anywhere." Fletch knelt and balanced the boxes carefully until they stood by themselves. "You two have been seeing each other. And now you've dropped in to see Mr. Matthews." Dad managed to laugh this time but it sounded like he was catching his breath. "The man I've worked for all my life."

"He was very interested in Henry's idea." Fletch was happy to tell Dad, "how to stop war."

"What war?" Dad asked me.

"Any war," I said.

"That's the beauty of it," Fletch pointed out. "Any two countries get into trouble, all they have to do is swap their life insurance. It works vice versa."

"No, that won't do." My father drew both hands down from his forehead, wiping his face. He held his eyes shut with his fingers and leaned with his elbows on the desk. "I think it might be better to start from the top, from the very beginning."

"Let me," I told Fletch. I went all the way back to the X15 and then described how the bomb shelter changed things and went on from there. For a while Dad kept his face covered. Then with a sigh he reached for a pad as I talked and started to make notes. Whatever it was he wrote he looked up and nodded at me now and then to keep me going. He appeared to be taking it all right, everything I told him.

Not me, though. Standing up there in my father's office, trying to talk above the screech of the wind and the pounding the building took as the gusts hit and turned off, I could hardly believe what I was saying. To myself, I didn't sound as if I was in my right mind.

It didn't seem possible that I could be talking about the two of us in the same breath, me and Mr. John F. Matthews, the President of American Lock and Locomotive. It had to be insane that I was the one who actually walked in on him in his own office.

Because all my life Mr. John F. Matthews was someone you were only supposed to hear about, along with George Washington and Santa Claus and Robinson Crusoe, without knowing whether he was real or just made up by your parents to explain how things had to be. He was always their last answer to any question I ever asked, like why we had to move, or the house we had to live in, or the people we had to visit on a Sunday afternoon. John F. Matthews was nothing you could do anything about. Except now I had.

It was hard getting through the last of what I had to tell my father, looking straight ahead through the Venetian blinds at the rolling gray that tore past in the high wind.

"What do you think, sir?" asked Fletch when I was done.

Dad looked up from his pad.

"About Henry Three's idea?" Fletch explained.

"It's a very good idea," said my father. "Ingenious."

"D'you hear that?" Fletch asked me. "And Mr. Matthews too," he pointed at the Action Memo on Dad's desk, "he got it in a flash. Doesn't he mention, sir, how much he liked it?"

Dad shoved the Memo across the desk for Fletch and me to look at. On top was printed MATTHEWS with a long line of initials down the side. One of them, HL II, was checked off. All that was scribbled on the paper was *"Hdle & Rpt."* It was nothing even that you could pronounce.

"Handle and report," Dad read it for us.

"So that's it," Fletch looked up. "But doesn't that mean sir, he likes it. If he asks you to handle Henry's idea and report on it?"

"What he wants me to handle," my father cleared his throat, "and report on is Henry Three. It's not every morning that the son of a Vice-President drops in on Mr. Matthews, Fletcher, to suggest that A. L. & L. discontinue part of its business.

"But he wanted to know how to stop wars," insisted Fletch.

"Who doesn't?" My father shook his head. "The fact remains, that's not the business we're in. The United Nations, it'd be more in their line, I imagine."

"The shelter though. He was going to take it back." Fletch stopped dead and slowly swallowed. "You mean it's no use? You mean Henry's wasted all that time besides the brain power he's put into this?"

"No." Dad wiped his face again and held it in both his hands, his elbows back on the desk. "He's done a lot worse than waste time. And I think, Fletcher, I'd like to speak to Henry privately for a few moments. If you don't mind."

Fletch held my arm and of all the people we'd heard that morning who were sorry none of them sounded anywhere near as bad as Fletch. "I'm sorry, Henry Three. Am I sorry!"

We were alone. I stood at the desk and Dad sat in his chair and we listened to the wind get worse. It piled into the Empire State so hard you could hear the jolt and feel the sway of it high up as we were. It was enough to scare you.

"Dad," I finally managed to tell him. "You don't have to tell me how terrible this is, what I've done. If there's any way I can make it up to you, anything. I'll do whatever you say. I don't care how long it takes. Years."

"Unfortunately," my father's hands dropped and he stared at me, "we don't have that kind of time, Henry Three. When one of these shows up," he reached across for the Action Memo, "it's a fire alarm in this company. Mr. Matthews expects a call back within half an hour, with some sort of response. Of what a man intends to do, at least."

"About handling me?"

"About the whole situation you've brought up. Henry!" He slammed the memo to his desk. "How in the name of Heaven could you ever pull a stunt like this?"

"I don't know, Dad." It was a more terrible mystery to me than it was to him. "The thought just came up somehow, the way we could get into Room 7820. And you couldn't help wonder, I guess, how it'd turn out. We must've just gone along with the thought and there we were."

"And there he sits, Mr. Matthews up there in 7820 wondering what kind of a man I am. What kind of a father. What must he be thinking, Henry?"

"I don't know."

"And by tomorrow morning it's going to be all over A. L. & L. How Lovering's kid fetched up in Matthews' office to tell him how to run the corporation. That's all it takes. Just one rolling laugh like that to start a landslide. One that'll carry me and your mother and you and all of us right over the edge."

"I know."

"How can Lovering run a Division of the company, that'll be the question when he can't manage his thirteen-year-old boy? What's the answer going to be?"

"But Dad, please. I don't know."

"Then you'd better find out." With one rigid finger Dad hammered on the Memo. "We've got a lifetime invested in this desk, Henry. It's you and me, this desk, and our entire family. It's our home in Crestview. It's your future. And by all the Saints," his finger collapsed, "you ought to know that by now." The way Dad's jaw tightened, you'd think a tooth would crack. "Maybe they're right, the whole new school that says we ought to get back to the old fashioned woodshed and the leather belt. To that old war cry, spare the rod and spoil the child. Maybe so. Maybe the only way you'll ever understand this is to get it beaten into you."

"I don't care. It's only what I have to expect."

"Well, that makes it mutual." Dad came out of his chair and around the desk and the room went black with the slap that hit. I ducked and the flat of his hand caught me again under the right eye. I banged into the desk, blind and trying to get away from the crush in my jaw and my nose clamped tight.

He steadied me, my father did, with a hand on my shoulder. He pushed me gently against a hard chair and I sat down. When I looked up at him, with the hurt flashing below my ear, he was filling a glass with water from a leather covered bottle on his desk. "So help me," he shook his head, "I never thought this would happen to us."

I couldn't take a chance, not for a couple of seconds, to tell him it was all right. He held the glass out to me.

"It's okay." I finally managed to let him know. And actually, that was the truth. The hurt there was made up somehow for how bad I felt. I was paid back a part at least for what I'd done to my father. "I don't need any water."

"Go ahead. Drink up, will you?" I managed to get half

a glass down. "I've never been through anything like this with you before," said Dad, "but water ought to help."

"I guess that's because we've never had any conversation like this before, this serious."

"No." My father took the glass and drank what was left. He didn't seem mad anymore, watching me, but he gripped the desk as he leaned against it to wait until it was all gone, the anger he'd felt. It took a little while and then the tight hold did loosen and his knuckles showed less white. "This is the first and last time for us, Henry. We can't let it come up like this ever again."

"Not as far as I'm concerned. I promise."

"And so do I. I promise too." He pushed my head back. "Are you going to make it?"

"No problem. It's fine."

He lifted up and sat on his desk, looking down at me. We breathed easier, both of us, and we listened to the high tearing noise of the wind. "Well," at last he rubbed his eyes, "I guess we'd better face it. The big problem. I'd better put in that call Mr. Matthews is waiting for."

And then a very strange thing happened. My father went to a corner of the office where one of the wood panels opened up, for a door. Inside there was a basin and a mirror with a light over it. Dad hung up his jacket and washed very carefully, combing his hair just right and getting the knot of his tie exactly in the middle. He rearranged the handkerchief in the breast pocket of his jacket when he put it on again and checked, twisting around, how he looked from the rear. I thought he had in mind all of a sudden to go up and visit Mr. Matthews. Instead he came back to his desk and sat down.

In front of him he arranged the pad with the notes he'd made and on one side two folders that he took from the drawer. "Well here we go," he made the remark to himself and he dialed. I'd never seen my father do anything like that before, I mean get all spruced up just to make a telephone call.

"Lovering, here," said Dad when Mr. Matthews got on the phone. And his voice was a surprise. It was pitched up, higher than I ever heard him speak. And he acted, Dad did, like he couldn't be happier. As if there were nothing in the world to be troubled about. He laughed.

"Of course, Mr. Matthews," Dad grinned into the phone, "I know you're not interested in the incident of the boy in itself. That's right, Henry's his name, same as my own. But I do wish you'd give me the chance to apologize and to tell you, sir, how much I regret that — ." I guess Mr. Matthews interrupted. Dad went quiet. He closed his eyes and felt at his forehead, nodding all the time.

"I get your point, Mr. Matthews, exactly. If the boy is a symptom of the general reaction to the Super Zero, of course you want the background. Naturally." Dad laughed, looking at the notes he'd made and pulling a paper from one of his folders. "As we all know sir, the critical problem of marketing the Zero line, as you've pointed out yourself, is the question of timing." Dad made a check against one of his notes. He told about the test shelters he had spotted around the country and the consumer research he was analyzing for a meeting next Tuesday.

I didn't understand half of what my father said. He mentioned about conflicting climates of opinion and the controversial factor and the index of international stability and he checked off each point he made against the notes on his pad.

But worse than that, I didn't understand my father. Keyed up as he was and nervous, he kept laughing and apologizing at everything that came along. In spite of the fix he was in, he kept trying for jokes. It didn't seem natural. Just to watch him smiling so hard and to listen to the strange voice he used, that began to be a lot worse than the ache spreading from my jaw. Talking to Mr. Matthews he didn't seem like my father at all, in any way that I ever remembered him. He sounded like a man who was cheerful and thankful, when all the while he seemed to be suffering. He was a man you had to be sorry for.

"You mean our own experience, sir, in Crestview?" Dad laughed. "Well, we never expected a high margin of community approval if you remember. Not during a period of normalcy. And we still haven't had the Zero with us long enough, Mr. Matthews, to check out the final factor of familiarity." Dad chuckled. "Even the early automobile was resented, if I can reach that far back, until the public became used to it." Dad checked off another point on his notes and he laughed again. "Oh no, sir, it's no insuperable problem for the family. We're holding up."

I never thought I'd hear my father come that close to lying. And then it got worse. They were talking about me. "Except for the boy, of course. Exactly Mr. Matthews, this morning's incident does show considerable anxiety on the boy's part. But frankly I have to admit that Henry's a rather special case. Normal enough, yes. But a little super-heated let's say, on the imaginative side." He nodded three or four times. "Well the fact is Henry's been brought up same as our others, with no psychological frills. I agree Mr. Matthews. I think you nailed it down in your Detroit speech, if you remember, the mention you made of the old fashioned wood shed and the leather belt."

I looked up at the words, the same ones exactly that Dad used when he explained things to me. Now it seemed they were only an idea that Mr. Matthews thought up.

Dad laughed. "Yes he's still here, sir. And I'm afraid the rod did get used, as you put it, where it would do the most good. No sir, thrashing a youngster does not come easy." And then Dad went ahead and checked off another point on his pad.

I twisted in my chair. I skipped a breath. He was no one you could feel sorry for any longer. Not now, when he was going into what no one had to hear about.

I knew for certain my Dad was mad enough when he slapped me so he couldn't help it. But just the same he made a note to mention it to Mr. Matthews, that he did. That didn't seem like a father either. When the first time it gets serious enough between us for him to swing at me, it helps to clear up a problem at the office. I never expected to run into anything like that.

I couldn't listen too well anymore or look at him. Everything that was private about us, all we said and how we felt, was getting mentioned as if it weren't so important after all. It was getting laughed at, the worst trouble he and I were ever in. Even with someone you just met you wouldn't think that'd happen. It was cold and strange and worse than being with a stranger.

Until it got hard to see where there was any actual connection between us, him and me, much less that he was anyone's father. Outside our names maybe, him being Henry Second and me being Henry Three. We were a couple of numbers you could count if that was any connection.

But if all we added up to was a little simple arithmetic, the two of us, it was just the same as not having a father at all. That's the way it came to feel up there in Room 7604.

16

"THAT'S FINE, MR. MATTHEWS. I CERTAINLY APPRECIATE the point of view you've adopted." Dad laughed and he hung up the phone. He swept up the Action Memo and he crumpled it. "That does it, Henry Three. We're out of the woods." He emptied his fist in the waste paper basket.

I didn't know what woods he was talking about. But it was just as well he was done with the trouble I'd caused him. On account of I was such a fool. Trying to think how to stop wars. So they'd take back the shelter. So we could stay in Crestview. I was a fool even to want to stay on in Crestview. What was the use of it? If where you ended up was with a man, high in an office somewhere, you couldn't even recognize for your own father. I don't know how I got to be that much of a fool, after taking it for granted for so many years, to find myself without a father.

175

One thing though, I wasn't going to end up in a place like this myself. If up here was where it got you, living in Crestview, there wasn't much point to it. Moving out of Crestview didn't matter anymore.

Dad watched me. "What's the trouble?"

I didn't have to answer, the banging came at the door. It was Caroline. "I'm afraid it's turned very serious, Mr. Lovering. The call's come through that everyone is excused as of immediately. To get home before the worst of the storm."

"Good idea," said Dad. "You get going."

She left Fletch standing behind her in the open door. "I don't want to break in on this but it's no time for a private talk, Mr. Lovering. The way it's been coming over your girl's radio out here, we're going to get the worst of it. I mean sir, Crestview is."

"Crestview?"

"The storm's kept shifting and the hurricane they were talking about, it's headed straight for Bayside now. That means us. Crestview."

"No!" Dad reached for the phone and started dialing.

"You ought to hear him, Henry, on the radio." Fletch pointed at the outside office. "He says a hurricane's more powerful than a hundred atom bombs. He sounds like the world's coming to an end."

"What if it is?"

Fletch stopped pointing. He quieted down. Then he came over to stand at the desk in front of my chair. "It was bad, huh? With your father?"

"With who?" I asked him.

"Look, I guess you got a right to be sore at me, for

176

dragging you into this. I know that."

"No one's sore at you, Fletch. For Heavens sake, not at you. You're a friend of mine, aren't you?"

"Well, if you put it that way. I guess I am," said Fletch.

The phone banged as my father finished talking to someone at the telephone company. "There's no way through to Crestview," he told us. "Every last line is down." He headed for the little door again where the sink was and reached in for his hat and raincoat. "Is there actually any lunch in those?" he pointed at the stack of boxes.

"Two pastramis," said Fletch. "One on a roll and besides a ham and cheese on rye."

"Then bring them along and you two can eat on the train. Henry!" he yelled at me.

"Yes sir."

"Come alive, Henry. Let's get out to your mother and sisters. If I know Ma she has them down in the shelter by now. But the faster we get out there, the better."

I couldn't see the reason for all the excitement, long as Ma and Sis and Lady were safe. And Fletch, he wasn't particularly concerned about his Grandfather, all the storms The Mansion had stood up to for so many years. But Dad was just as excited as everyone else going down in the elevator.

It wasn't like when we came up, no one talking. Now they were all comparing what they'd heard about the storm. It was called Holy Hannah because every hurricane is named after a girl. And along with Hannah the radio was calling this one 'Holy' because it was turning out to be such a terror. Everyone in the elevator gave different reports about how fast the wind was traveling, up to eighty miles an hour. But with all the excitement no one seemed worried especially or scared, the way they'd been all morning before there was anything to get frightened at so far as I could see. Now the worst that got mentioned seemed to make everyone happier, to listen to the women giggle.

As bad as the wind when it hit you outside was the noise, the roar in the streets. There wasn't any chance for a cab, the few cars that went by. The three of us hugged the fronts of the stores. The pavement ahead was solid water that raced in the wind and boiled in the pelting rain. You couldn't hear yourself think. Which was all right with me, what I had to think about.

I went down when he hit and my head cracked Larkin below the knees. Fletch sprawled across the sidewalk and I ended up with Dad on top of me, half smothered in his rain coat, but no more hurt than I was before. It was a low block Dad hit me with, his shoulder doubling me up. When he pulled us into the doorway of a shoe store, I saw why. Along with the scattered lunch Fletch dropped there was a steel box on the sidewalk, cracked and turning over, leaving a trail that was bits of metal and machinery.

"Someone's air conditioner," Dad yelled. "Ripped out of a window upstairs. Will you stop dreaming, Henry," he pulled us to our feet. "That could've been for keeps!"

I guess it was a pretty narrow miss Dad saved us from. It was strange watching him as he brushed at the smear that ran down his raincoat, after the way I'd seen him in his office. He wasn't keyed up at all or nervous anymore, in spite of all the dangers he warned us about. In a way he even seemed pleased with the storm.

And that was what you noticed about the crowds at Penn

Station. No one was walking along anymore wrapped up in the secret worries that bothered him. They all seemed pleased, wherever you looked. As if the hurricane were a big affair that no one got left out of because he didn't have an invitation. You couldn't help be surprised at the sudden change.

And that went for the ones from Crestview too. Mr. Feddersen was the first we came across. I didn't give him a second look, seeing I hadn't even passed the time of day with his boy Pete for the last week. And right that moment I didn't care if I ever saw anyone from Crestview again. And Fletch of course, he didn't expect any conversation. Nor Dad either, since he and Feddersen gave up playing bridge together on the train every night. So we just kept shoving our way through the jam.

"Lovering," Feddersen reached for Dad. "Were you able to get through on the phone?"

"The line's out," Dad yelled back.

"I tried for an hour," Feddersen bellowed. "Every telephone pole in the area must be down."

"Feddersen!" It was Mr. Sattersley in the crowd. "Hank!" he yelled at Dad. "It's just come through on the radio." He couldn't fight closer than a dozen feet. "They're got a new fix on Holy Hannah. Straight for Crestview. We're sitting right in the middle of the alley."

"Heaven help us!" bawled Feddersen.

"The gusts are up to eighty," yelled Dad.

"Ninety," Mr. Sattersley topped him. "And there's still two hours before the worst hits us."

"Three," came a roar from the back. It was Mr. Driscoll shaking a ruined umbrella over his head. "Three hours to go. And already she's worse than Carol back in fifty-five."

It was peculiar, if you cared to take notice, how they behaved. You'd think none of us ever stopped being the best of friends. Driscoll started to tell us about his wrecked umbrella and Dad described about the air conditioner, when the gate to the Bayside train opened and the crowd of us got carried along. We picked up Mr. Klein as we went and down on the platform getting on the train, Mr. Simpson.

We ended up in the lounge car with a bar in it that was packed, most of the men reaching for drinks past the ones in front. And for all the conversation about how terrible Holy Hannah was, everyone seemed in fine spirits. Dad along with the others. It was just as well he had the rest of them to talk to seeing there was nothing, if we were alone, that he and I had to say to each other.

There wasn't even much I could tell Fletch when he kept asking what happened in my father's office. "Okay," he said after a while. "I guess it's none of my business. But you ought to stop worrying about it, Hank. We're heading into the middle of a hurricane."

"What difference does it make?"

"It could only blow Crestview straight off the map."

"Isn't that what you and your grandfather want," I asked him. "So you can put the place back into potatoes?"

Fletch suddenly smiled. "Yes," he said.

"That'd be fine with me too," I tried to tell him.

But there wasn't much chance for conversation in the roar. Even after the first couple of stops when the crowd eased off, the yelling stayed loud on account of the noise outside and all the pocket radios going. There was nothing

180

you could see through the windows, plastered deep with water. Above the storm every so often you heard a hollow crash and felt the car shudder. The word was we were getting hit with stuff that was flying. The train went slower and slower and finally it stopped altogether.

The conductor came running through. The men at the bar caught him. "We may have to go back to Stony Point," he yelled. "He's leery, the engineer is, about making it across the Broad Neck cutoff coming up." That's a place where there was a high banked track across the swamp. The engineer suspected the roadbed might be washed out with the big tide that was getting blown in from the bay.

No one wanted to go back. There was no way to get home from Stony Point. Except by car and taxi and all the radios were yelling how no cars were allowed on any roads.

"So we can't go back to Stony Point," Mr. Sattersley yelled at the conductor. "We've got families to get to, all of us."

"I've got a train to run." The conductor kept waving to free himself. "Do you know what we're up against? There's buildings getting turned over down the line. Buildings on their own foundations, not running on a track where a buckle could send us over, or an extra heavy gust. It's no use, gentlemen."

"Just a minute." It was my Dad who answered the conductor. "Mr. Sattersley's right. There's a couple of hundred men on this train who have to get home. You'd better make up your mind you're going to take us there."

"I can't. I've been with this company twenty-eight years, a perfect record. Where am I going to end up if I lose a trainful of people?"

"You don't get the idea." My father talked just as matter of fact as if he were sitting down to dinner. "You're not running this train any more. It belongs to us."

"My train?"

Dad found a paper in his pocket and went to writing on it. "It's our train now. We're taking over," he looked up. "All you have to do is keep it moving. Here," he offered the paper to the conductor, "you've got a perfectly legal receipt from your train, from me. And maybe," he looked around, "there's others would like to sign?" All the yelling went on, it seemed everyone was ready to put his name down. "There you are," Dad smiled at the conductor. "You'll have a list of more than a hundred witnesses, none of them friendly, that you couldn't do anything else except keep moving. That protects you," Dad pointed out. "So let's get out of here."

"It's mutiny," Fletch stared at me. "Your Dad can't take away their railroad train!"

But that's what he did. Everyone backed Dad up, reaching to write their names on his paper. There was no way for the conductor or even the engineer, I guess, to stand up to so many men. The conductor gave up.

"Whatever you say Cap," he shrugged at Dad and started out. "It's your funeral."

The conductor was wrong about the rank because it was a Major Dad made in the Marines, before I was born. Not that it mattered. The crowd cheered Dad when the train started moving ahead again.

"You never mentioned," Fletch shook his head at me, "what a cool customer your father is. He's running the 3:37! What do you think of that?"

Personally, I didn't know what to think. Dad certainly

wasn't the same man I watched talking to Mr. Matthews not an hour before. There was no comparison. My trouble was that I never had too much experience with my father, where he had to deal with anything important, to know all about him. I guess it was the way I saw him up in his office, though, that's what you mostly had to expect. Considering all the time he put in, up at the office.

Except right now I had to admit he handled things cool enough. He unlatched the vestibule door and when it flew open that gave him a chance for a look, now and then, at how we were doing. When we came to the cutoff, the swamp was gone. The water was up to within a foot of the tracks. There wasn't much air, according to Dad, just flying water that peeled off the big rollers coming in, driving at us along with the rain.

We made it past Broad Neck and the noise changed from the hammering of the spray back into the pounding of the wind. We headed into the last curve that would bring us to Crestview.

Dad turned from the vestibule and yelled for Mr. Klein. I looked around the corner through the open door and saw a big yellow sedan traveling along the highway with a woman driving. It was a yellow Cadillac same as belonged to Gardner Klein's family. And it was in trouble, whipped by the wind and weaving with all the speed it was making.

Before Mr. Klein showed up, it happened. A part of a tree came out of nowhere. It slammed the front of the car. The yellow Cadillac started to twist sideways, skidding through a highway marker. And so slow you wanted to put out your hand to hold it, the big car came off the shoulder of the highway and turned over into a ledge of rock where it crumpled to a stop with its wheels up, spinning.

Dad came to his feet and pulled the leather cord overhead, the emergency brake that locked the train into a sliding stop. Mr. Feddersen came running with Mr. Klein who took one look out the door and yelled "No!" again and again. "No!"

Fletch and I followed the three men out. The choking blast we stepped into filled your throat with so much air you couldn't breathe. We backed our way after the men until Dad stopped us.

"It's not their car. Not Klein's," Dad held us back. "It wasn't Mrs. Klein." We turned at the sound of the train. It pulled away without us. But we were close enough to Crestview. We were okay, long as it wasn't Gardner's mother under all that twisted machinery.

"It's another lady." Dad shoved us behind a boulder where there was a little protection. "It's nothing to look at." He took off his raincoat and started away. "She's dead."

We pressed against the cracked face of the stone and I watched the puddle at my feet. It was like a basin under a faucet with the water pouring down off the highway and past the wrecked car. As I watched, the puddle started to turn red.

17

I<small>T WAS STRANGE AT THE</small> C<small>ADILLAC AFTER</small> D<small>AD COVERED</small>
up what was inside with his raincoat. Mr. Klein wouldn't
come with us, not until he pushed off into the pouring wind
to stand by himself. He prayed. Or at least he crossed himself. But whether it was for the lady he never knew or to
give thanks she wasn't his wife, there was no way to tell.
And in the middle of it the Cadillac joined in. The horn
must've shorted from the driving wet and it wailed up and
down. We left it still crying behind us, the crushed yellow
car, as we climbed our way into Crestview.

That's how it felt, as if we were pulling ourselves up
a mountain, crouching far into the wind with each step that
we took. I had to keep swallowing all the time to clear my
ears, same as being up high. It was on account of the
sudden low pressure. Helping each other to climb, us five

were the only ones moving against the storm. I saw Winner, Shep Untermeyer's dog, racing the other way or getting blown before the wind toward the meadows along the shore.

It was almost dark by the time we reached Crestview. The clouds packed close overhead to shut out the day that still held to the far edge of wherever you looked. And the light that was left made the town look sick, the greenish tinge it had. The roofs were swept clean, with no T.V. antennas. The trees were gone. The air was filled with whatever you can imagine, flying roof tiles and brick and timber and even someone's rocker.

There was no telling what hit Mr. Feddersen. He was a knocked-out huddle blowing into a flattened hedge by the time Dad reached him. Dad lifted him through the exploded picture window of an empty house. I couldn't look at Mr. Feddersen's shoulder when Dad pulled his shirt off, crushed and with a piece of bone curved in blood. But Mr. Feddersen didn't make a sound when he came to. His face went set, that's all, and he drank from a bottle of whiskey that Dad found, as if it were water. Dad got Feddersen's shoulder into a bandage with stuff from a medicine cabinet. It was unexpected how fast Dad worked and how gentle.

We packed Feddersen for safety into a fireplace with cushions and rugs and the whiskey bottle until we could fetch a doctor.

We didn't have a real doctor closer than Bayside. In Crestview there was only Doctor Mindell. He was a psychiatrist whose office was in New York City, same as everyone else. We were lucky enough to find him crowded under his own grand piano, but he wasn't much help. Dr. Mindell described how he was a specialist in mental disorders and, far as he could see, Mr. Feddersen's troubles weren't mental. Under the circumstances Dr. Mindell perferred to stay put under the piano and take care of his own problem which was mental. He was scared.

Dad and Mr. Klein crept under the piano after him. There was no way to hear what the three of them shouted at each other, face to face. But Dr. Mindell was persuaded to go have a look at Feddersen with Mr. Klein holding tight to his arm.

Dad led Fletch and me on toward our house, crawling over telephone poles and moving dumps of furniture. There were a lot of crying automobiles in Crestview too, some on their sides with their horns blowing. Once Dad had to haul Fletch away from a snarl of electric cables whipping across the street, throwing sparks and jumping blue flames in the growing dark.

We were working our way past the Driscolls' when the front door flew open and we saw someone inside. And that's where we found them, a crowd of women and children down in the basement. Ma was there along with Sis and Lady.

When we came down though it was like the whole crowd was our family. Dad was the first husband to show up. The ones on the train got held up at the wrecked railroad station. And the sight of a full grown man, I guess, gave everyone the feeling they were rescued. Dad got hugged and cried over. It happened to me and even Fletcher too. There was no question were we anyone's friend or not. Even the ones from the X15, Ray and Pete and Gardner, charged us like we were brothers. And the truth is, coming in from the murdering storm outside I was never happier to see any bunch of people. Just the sight of them raised the hope that, with all of us together, we'd make out.

That's the way Ma explained it, holding tight to Dad while she kept a grip on the back of my head. It was Ma who helped Mrs. Driscoll to gather the wives to face whatever was coming until the men showed up. Even though the shelter was safer, Ma couldn't stand being down there alone with Sis and Lady. Dad understood, how you wanted to be with someone else when the worst comes, so you could share how you felt.

And there wasn't any secret how we all felt. We were scared. Even in the Driscoll basement minutes went by when the house shook like a plane taking off and you thought the roof had to let go. Scared was the most honest thing you could be. It changed people. Once we got honest with each other, a good many of us turned out a lot different from what you'd expect.

Like Mrs. Feddersen when she heard about her hubsand. Mrs. Feddersen's hardly any bigger than her son Pete and very elegant always in the way she acts and dresses. But she could've been a steam fitter, the language she used when Dad tried to keep her from rushing out to get to her husband. She called Dad names I never heard before. He had to let her go, finally, with a couple of older boys to hold on to her.

But the one most changed was my own father. Especially after the morning we'd spent together when he didn't seem like any father at all. There had to be some mistake about that, the way he behaved in his office. Nothing worried him now. It felt safe just to be with my father. And that's the feeling everyone else had, I guess. Even after the other men showed up, most of the managing got left up to Dad.

It wasn't long before he had the Driscoll house organized, with most of the windows on the storm side boarded up and those on the other, along with the doors, left open to the thundering wind. That was to equalize the pressure so the roof wouldn't get sucked off. He chose the ones to handle the water seeping in and to get food started and sent out parties to check those houses where there might be other women and kids still on their own. With all he had to do, I was proud when Dad noticed me.

But I wasn't really sure about him and me, whether he was the stranger he seemed or my father for real, until we got over to the Andrews house on Dorchester Avenue. Warren Andrews who used to date Sis showed up begging for help to reach his mother who was trapped in the flooded cellar of their house. The only ones who could go were Dad and Mr. Driscoll and we were allowed to come along, Fletch and me, to lend a hand.

All that part of Dorchester Avenue was under water, six or seven inches of it. There wasn't only the blast to face and the cutting rain but the water in the street that came at you like rapids. There were houses ripped open. The Andrews place was whole but it leaned. Warren's Ma had been caught in the basement when the house shifted and now, with the water pouring in, there wasn't much time to get to her. There wasn't much way to get to her either, only a hole in the foundation that was too small for Dad or Mr. Driscoll to get through. I could make it though.

"No!" Dad shoved me back. "Stay out of this."

"But listen to her." There were screams down the cellar you could hear even above the storm. After all the chances

Dad had been taking, I had to try at least. "I can get to her."

"Not you." Dad tightened his arm around my neck and shouted with his face close to mine. "This whole place could go. With the both of you. You can't go in."

"Why not?"

"What do you mean, why not? I'm your father, Henry Three. And I love you. That's why not!"

It came sudden as the slap that hit me in his office. He'd never said anything like that before, my father. There were only inches between us. And nowhere to look except into my father's eyes. I knew he meant what he said. I knew what happened that morning at American Lock and Locomotive, that couldn't be the truth. What was honest came now when we kneeled in the mud and water together against the Andrews house with the roaring around us and the heavy rain. I was sure this was the truth what my father told me because that's the way I felt too, as far as he was concerned.

I couldn't keep looking at my father. I was afraid it would show, when there was no way to save Mrs. Andrews, how happy I was. And then behind my father I saw it was Fletch instead who was crawling backwards through the hole with the help of Warren Andrews into the cellar below. I scrambled after him, yelling to Fletch to come back.

Mr. Driscoll pushed me away. "Beat it!" he shouted at me. "Drag your tail out of here!"

"It could all come down on top of him, the whole house."

"No it won't, son. Let him be!"

"Who says it won't?"

"Me. I say so. Didn't I put in the best six years of my life propping the whole world up over my head? I'll take care of him."

It was hard to believe but Mr. Driscoll turned out to be the best hard rock miner that ever hauled copper out of the State of Arizona! He told me so himself.

It was starting to look as if everyone in Crestview was as bad as me. The way I did with my I.Q. they were all hiding who they really were. It wasn't only my father who was telling the truth for the first time. There was Mr. Driscoll too, who was supposed to be a banker considering how important he was at Manufacturer's Trust Company. But he was actually a first class miner, Mr. Driscoll was, now the truth came out. You rarely see a man as proud as when he showed me the UMW card that made him a member of the United Mine Worker's Union, for life.

It was Mr. Driscoll, once Fletch hoisted Mrs. Andrews to safety on top of the furnace, who figured the way to get her out. There weren't any tools for making the hole to the cellar any bigger. Instead Mr. Driscoll put us to work with a couple of automobile jacks, their handles lengthened by long pieces of pipe to give us better leverage. He and Warren handled one while Dad and I paired up on the other. The idea was to lift the wall of the house right off it's foundations. And it worked.

At least the jacks lifted seven or eight notches with me hauling face to face with Dad until my teeth clamped. Every little bit we gained, one of the men would shove timber into the space we opened. Even so the jacks finally buckled under the weight, cracking up the cement-block below. Which turned out just as well. All we had to do was get rid of the cracked cement and we had the size hole we needed.

The biggest trouble in rescuing Mrs. Andrews turned out to be Mrs. Andrews herself. She wouldn't come out of the cellar without her sable coat which was sunk somewhere in five feet of water. Dad slipped into the cellar and came back neck deep, carrying Mrs. Andrews toward the hole. She kept punching and screaming at Dad to stop.

"I'm not getting out of here. Not without my sable." Mrs. Andrews braced herself against the sides of the hole, arms stiff. "That's all I've got. That's all I am. Please! I can't go without my sable."

It was Larkin who found the coat, fetching below water underneath the ruined staircase. He brought it to us, pulling himself along by an overhead beam. It was only then that Mrs. Andrews let herself be saved. And once we got her into the Driscoll basement Ma and Mrs. Untermeyer took care of the fur coat like it was something wounded, wringing it out and brushing it. That seemed the best treatment you could give Mrs. Andrews who went on blessing them until she fell asleep, exhausted.

But no one gave it any notice, how Mrs. Andrews thought she was nothing but her own fur coat. Just as there wasn't any mention when Mrs. Feddersen turned into a steam-fitter or Mr. Driscoll proved he was a hard rock miner. It seemed everyone expected you'd be different now we were all honest with each other. And no one seemed to mind particularly, whatever it was you turned out to be.

There was even a good deal of sympathy for Dr. Mindell when he showed up after taking care of Mr. Feddersen. He came to apologize to everyone, to explain that no doctor had the right to be scared even though he did get dominated by his older sister Martha, Dr. Mindell told us, until he was four years old. It didn't make sense to me. But there were a lot who told Dr. Mindell they understood, and that got him calmed down.

That was the thing about Holy Hannah. Everyone cared about you no matter what went wrong. I guess it was a surprise for all of us my age, the way we got to see our parents in such a new way. They were brave, some of our fathers and mothers, and strong and they went to pieces, some did, and couldn't stop complaining or they took to drinking a good deal. But all together there didn't seem anything they couldn't handle.

Crestview was supposed to be only vice-presidents and brokers and agents and lawyers, all executives. But during Holy Hannah they fixed the plumbing in the toilet and got gasoline stoves started, they turned into carpenters and lumberjacks and worked out electrical circuits. They nursed each other and did the cooking and showed us card tricks and joined into a choir. They were wonderful.

Holy Hannah was wonderful. That's something hard to admit. But before it came along I didn't seem to have any father. And then there he was, a man I couldn't be prouder about who even said he loved me. Before I didn't have a home, none I cared about. And then I found myself belonging to a crowd of people, strange as they were, who couldn't be finer. No matter how bad it was, that's the truth about Holy Hannah. It was good, too.

And no one knows better than I do how bad Holy Hannah really was, after what happened when the "eye" came over Crestview.

That's what they call the center of a hurricane, the dead calm middle of it that the winds blow around, the eye. When it came we all began shouting at each other. That was only because of the sudden quiet down in the basement where we'd been yelling for so long to make ourselves heard. You could look around too in the light that came from the little windows. In the eye it was still daytime.

Outside it was like the end of a fine afternoon with the sun starting to set. It was warmer than I remembered and heavy with a strange smell that could be escaping gas. There were lots of birds. It was someone's idea that the birds were blown into the center of the storm and flew along with the eye as it moved. It was peculiar in the middle of Holy Hannah, almost as frightening as the storm itself.

Fletch went off, now he had a chance to get to The Mansion on his own. The rest of us went to work in the half hour we had boarding up the windows on the other side of the Driscoll house because the winds, when the hurricane started to blow again, would be coming from the opposite direction.

"Shep!" I heard Mr. Untermeyer. "Shep!" He was yelling for his smallest boy who'd come out with us. "Shep!"

It reminded me how I tried to quiet Shep when we first showed up in the basement. The redhead was crying because he had to leave his dog Winner behind, when his mother grabbed him to rush for the Driscolls. I described to Shep where we'd seen Winner, how his dog was okay.

"Do you think Shep might've set out to look for him?" I asked Mr. Untermeyer. "To find Winner?"

"Where?" Mr. Untermeyer held me. "Shep doesn't know this storm isn't over. He'll get caught."

Dad let me go with Mr. Untermeyer to show where we'd last spotted the racing dog. I ran, climbing over the wrecks of houses and I found myself saying out loud, "Please!" with the hope of catching sight of the seven-year-old. But when we came into the open country there was nothing moving except the birds in the sky and the rolling water that flooded across the fields that were low.

"Where was it?" Mr. Untermeyer's grip stopped me. "Where'd you see the dog. Think, Henry, try to remember."

Even if I could find the spot exactly there was no telling where Winner had got to by now. We could only run and change direction and keep on running until the water chopped up in the winds that started again. It grew darker.

"We're losing him." Mr. Untermeyer kept running. "It's getting too late."

It was when the rains came back, sweeping sheets that spread across the sunken meadows, I thought I heard barking. Mr. Untermeyer was sure of it and he headed toward the shore where the waves broke white. I heard it again, a high yelping off to my right. I yelled for Mr. Untermeyer plowing up ahead. He didn't hear me. I turned off on my own.

Up on a rise there was a tree splintered and another with its roots half out of the water. It was from there I saw Winner. He was on an island across a two acre pond jumping stiff legged as if at the end of a leash, barking at what was in the water. I couldn't see anything. Until I climbed the trunk of the tree.

It was a hand. Then the redheaded crew cut of a second grade kid. It was Shep and with every part of me I yelled his name. "Shep!" I got rid of my slicker and kicked the sneakers off my feet. I dove shallow as I could and hit mud.

It wasn't deep enough to drown in. "Get on your feet!"

I yelled at Shep. "Get up!" I shoved against the water never higher than my chest. I swam to move faster. But when I reached where I'd spotted, he was nowhere around. I dove, reaching into the mud and then I had a fistful of cloth. It twisted as I stood up.

Shep was heavy. I carried him through the water and he didn't hear that it was all right now, that there was nothing to be afraid of now. His face hung away from me.

Mr. Untermeyer came wading toward us. And I knew from the sight of the full grown man who cried soft as a tired baby that there was no way to save Shep. Mr. Untermeyer took his boy from me. He laid him on the ground and kneeled above him. Then Mr. Untermeyer started, leaning hard on the boy's ribs and lifting, carrying the boy's arms over the head, up and then down. I crawled from the water and kneeled in the mud. I watched the quiet crying man go on and on, until bending and straightening became a prayer the father was afraid to bring to an end.

There was a lick on my face. It was Winner. I held on to the dog and watched Mr. Untermeyer in the rain that was pounding again and in the wind that started to scream. Mr. Untermeyer came to an end. He hid the body of his son in his raincoat and crawled with him to the lifted roots of the tree. He huddled there and his face was hidden. But still, he rocked back and forth.

I remembered there was one last thing I had to do for Shep Untermeyer. I took his dog Winner to our bomb shelter, the way I promised.

18

It was quiet down there. Our shelter was the one place in Crestview that was quiet and warm and had its own light. The noise of the storm was far away and the only sound was Winner behind me when sometimes he whimpered.

Then the dog barked as the storm came back. It was my father who let himself in.

"Your Ma was right." Dad closed out the crash of Holy Hannah. "She was sure you'd be here."

I stayed with my face against the wall of the bunk. "We know about it. Everything." Dad sat down next to me. "They brought Mr. Untermeyer in." He felt across my shoulders and down the middle of my back. "So we know."

It was good to hear him, the soft way he spoke. I realized then I'd been waiting for him. There had to be someone I could tell about Shep Untermeyer, the part no one knew except me. It was too hard to keep down for much longer, the thought that kept turning colder and colder as I looked at the wall.

My father hauled me around and carefully he pulled off my shirt and peeled down the wet trousers and socks. He folded the blanket around me and it covered my head. The dark was nothing you minded long as Dad kept a tight hold and we sat together with Winner in the bunk. When he let go of me my father found a box of tissues in the cabinet above the stove. He gave me two pieces and put the box where I could help myself.

A whine came out of Winner and Dad patted him. "Maybe he's hungry?" Dad asked me.

"Maybe."

"Well, this is enough of an emergency to break out an emergency can of corned beef. Don't you think?"

"I think so."

Dad opened the locked closet and found a can. He twisted the top off and spread the corned beef on a white metal plate. Winner was very hungry, so much he yelped between bites. He was happy as ever. That was hard to understand. except a dog maybe can't realize too well. I turned back to the wall again, inside the blanket.

"Please," my father asked me. "Stick around, Henry." He sat and slowly shook me by the shoulder. "There's no use thinking about this. It's no one's fault."

From the dark where I was, I had to tell my father. He was the one person in the world I could talk to, after everything that had come up between us. "I think it is," I said. "I think it is someone's fault."

"No, Henry." Dad's hand on my shoulder got heavy. "Mr. Untermeyer told us no one could've tried harder than you, or done better."

"I could've done better."

"How?"

"If only I kept my promise to Shep." I pulled the blanket harder around me. "I gave him my word, I promised I'd bring Winner down here into the shelter when the worst came."

"What worst?"

"Like the atom bomb. And this is just as bad, isn't it?"

"Suppose it is."

"Then it was me. I saw Winner when we were coming into Crestview. It was up to me to get the dog and bring him down here. If I had, nothing would've happened to Shep. He'd be all right, Shep would," I was able to tell my father, "if it wasn't for me."

"No he wouldn't." My father was positive. "You couldn't have saved Shep that way."

"Why not?"

"I wouldn't have let you." It was too strong to hold back from, the pull that turned me over so I had to look up at my father. "You didn't have a chance of chasing after Winner back there. I'd never let you go. Two steps and I'd have had you by the back of the neck. What kind of a father do you think I am?"

He didn't give me a chance to tell him. "Do you think I'd let any boy of mine go climbing off into a hundred mile an hour hurricane. By himself?"

"No. I guess not."

"Guess? Of course not. And certainly I'd never go off

201

with you myself at that point, to run after a dog. Before we'd even found your mother or the girls.

"I guess you wouldn't."

"The whole thing was out of your hands. None of this was up to you. So how can it be your fault?"

"Maybe it isn't. Is that what you think?"

"Of course it isn't." My father lifted me half way up by the shoulders. "You're in a hurricane, son. By now you see how terrible it can be. Shep hurts, I know how you feel about Shep. But don't let's pile up the torture, thinking about fault. This was no one's fault." He let me down. "And certainly not yours, Henry. Not you."

I lay there looking up at him. "Thanks for explaining it. I'm glad," I told him, "that it wasn't on account of me." But I didn't feel glad. No matter how well I understood my father, Shep was gone. Whose fault it was didn't make any difference. It was good to be with my father and to talk with him in the shelter where it was quiet, but even with him around it wasn't any better, how I couldn't help feeling. "There's something wrong," I said and I went back into the dark of the blanket again, up against the wall.

"What is it, son?" my father asked. "What's wrong?"

"Me. There's something wrong with me," I tried to explain. "The way I think."

"About what?"

"Holy Hannah. I know you're right when you say how terrible it is. But part of it's good, too. That's the way it is in my mind. So what's wrong with me?"

"I'm sure there's nothing wrong with you," my father spoke very quietly. "But what good do you see in this disaster we're in?"

"There's the people for instance. They're good. They're a lot better than I imagined. They're changed. Everything is. Even you. You're changed."

"Me?"

"You're different since the storm. You're fine. Long as you just asked me what kind of a father you are, all I can say is you're about the best I ever ran into."

"I am?" My father leaned into the wall where he could look down at me. "When did you find that out? Just since the start of the storm?"

"Yes sir," I told him. "But I'm sure it's true."

"Are you though?" There was a sudden smile he had. "It's good to hear you're so positive about it."

"Especially over on Dorchester Avenue, I know that was true. The remark you made?"

"Which one?"

"When you mentioned about me. Don't you remember? How you felt as far as I was concerned?"

"That I loved you. Of course, Henry Three. I've always loved you."

"Yes. But the point is, it never came up before that I remember."

"It did, Henry. Back some." My father disappeared from up above. "When you were a good deal smaller." I just about heard him through the blanket. "Lately there hasn't been much chance to go into it."

"Not for me," I reminded him. "Not over there on Dorchester Avenue. I never did get the chance to tell you how I felt. I mean as far as you're concerned."

"How's that?"

"Well, just about the same."

The mattress creaked as my father got to his feet. After that it was still in the shelter except for the banging of the plate that Winner was licking. I lifted my head around the edge of the blanket to see what my father was up to. He was standing there, studying me, with that same smile. He shook his head. "No Henry Three, I wouldn't say there was anything wrong with you."

"But all I've told you, what I've been thinking, it seems to me good."

"Good doesn't cover it, to my mind. It's wonderful."

"That's how I feel. It's wonderful. But it's wrong, Dad. It's got to be wrong!"

"How, Henry? Please tell me."

"Why does it take something that can kill you, a kid who can't even swim yet, before it gets wonderful?"

My father didn't move. But his smile left as he watched me. Finally, he shook his head. "You can't let what happened to Shep Untermeyer destroy the good you've found, Henry. About you and me for instance. They're separate, those things. There's no connection between them."

"Except Holy Hannah. She's the reason for both, that's the connection. If there wasn't any hurricane, it wouldn't be wonderful. But Shep, he'd still be alive."

"Yes." My father glanced down to Winner and he bent to pat the dog. Winner braced himself over the empty plate and growled. "That does happen to be the case." My father straightened.

"Then it's right, the way I've been thinking?"

"Yes." My father took a seat on the bunk opposite. "You're right," he told me. "We are different, all of us. We have changed. We had to. Holy Hannah can change

204

us because she can kill us. It's only when we're forced, I don't now why, that we turn ourselves into something new. Once there's a chance we can get killed, we have to start living the best way we know how."

"That's your idea too?"

"Not mine, Henry. It's simply a fact. It came to me in the service, under combat. Under fire you find yourself looking at the world in a new way, at a cloud or even a blade of grass as if you were seeing it for the first time. Because is might be for the last time too. There are moments when you couldn't feel more alive because someone close by couldn't be more dead. You're ashamed that you feel so good."

"Same as here, same as Holy Hannah?"

My father nodded. "You haven't found out anything new."

"But it shouldn't be like that," I tried to get my father to see.

"No," he agreed with me. "If the only time we can get to feel better than ourselves is when it's dangerous, if the only time the world gets to look so wonderful is when it's blowing up around us, you're certainly right Henry. It shouldn't be like that."

"But isn't there something, Dad, you can do about it?"

"I wouldn't know. You've walked into a secret that no one wants to do anything about. That's the way we share the wars we've been in, me and the rest of the fathers here in Crestview, as if it were a deep secret. Of another way to live, more exciting and better than it is here day after day. There's almost the hope that another one might come along."

"Another war?"

"Or a Holy Hannah. Same thing. For a day that explodes all over the place, so we have to start living as best we can. That's the way it is, Henry. You've found something that shouldn't be and it can't be helped."

We watched Winner in the bunk across the way, with his nose under his back legs. Almost to prove what a good sleeper he was, Winner stretched and pushed his front paws stiff without waking up.

"But it's not you, son. There's nothing wrong with you, how you think and how you feel. You know that now, don't you?"

"Except there ought to be some way it could be wonderful," I found a piece of tissue to use, "without the rest of it. Without Shep."

"Give it time." My father lifted me to my feet on the edge of the bunk so that I was higher than he was. He hugged me and there was no way I could manage to hold on to him, caught the way my arms were underneath the blanket. "That's what time is for, Henry. No matter how hard we try to hang on to Shep, he's leaving us from one day to the next. The time will come when he'll be gone. And then we'll be left. I'll know I have a son I can be proud of. And you'll know, I promise you, that you have a father." He lifted me back to where I'd been sitting in the bunk. "Okay?"

"Okay," I agreed.

He leaned alongside my chin. "I'm getting back to the Driscolls to tell your mother you're doing fine." He reached for his rain coat and started to buckle up. "I can tell her that, can't I?"

"Yes sir," I said.

19

BUT THE TRUTH IS, MY FATHER MADE A MISTAKE DOWN
there in the shelter. When he said I found something that
shouldn't be, that I couldn't help. Because in Holy Hannah,
Shep Untermeyer wasn't the only one. It happened to Mr.
Larkin, Fletcher's Grandfather, too. And there was a great
deal I could do to help about that.

It was on account of the tree, the big oak tree the
Larkins had been growing for three hundred years. It
started to shift early in Holy Hannah and the roots of it
began to work loose. There was no chance for the tree
to bend, old as it was and rigid. And it was a disaster for
Mr. Larkin, according to Louie who works for them, to
watch the tree go.

Fletcher's Grandfather was sure that all that had to be
done was to tighten the turnbuckles, to take in the slack of

the whipping guy wires that held the tree up. Louie couldn't hold the old gentleman back. He went out with Mr. Larkin, fighting through the terrible wind and the drowning rain and the two of them went to work on the buckles with a crowbar. There was no way of breaking through the rust that held the big screws tight. And when the tree cracked, Louie ran.

Mr. Larkin couldn't make it, though, away from the falling tree. He was caught. Fletcher's grandfather was crushed and twisted by the heavy trunk that rolled over him. He was dead when Louie dragged him clear.

It all happened before Fletch showed up.

He sat by his Grandfather's bedside for the rest of Holy Hannah, Fletch did, and all through the night that came. He never talked or even answered Louie.

Everyone in Crestview learned about it the next morning. Louie was a little hard to understand because his English, which was never so good, went all to pieces from the way he felt about Mr. Larkin. His biggest worry, Louie explained, was for Fletcher. He didn't know what would happen now the boy was alone. That's what Louie wanted to talk about, all during the hours of the long night but Fletch never listened to anything that was said.

Louie did what he could on his own. The only relative he ever heard of that the Larkins had was a lady out in Los Angeles, a second cousin. He found her telephone number up in Grandpa Larkin's desk and sometime after midnight he made it into Bayside, which was the nearest any telephone was working. He had to walk the twelve miles because no car could drive along the piled-up roads. And toward morning Louie came back to The Mansion with good news.

He told Fletch there was nothing to worry about. The second cousin wanted to do everything she could to fix things. She was anxious for Fletch to come out and live with her own family, three girls and one boy, and was making all arrangements so that Fletcher would be happy. Louie was at least relieved, once he knew that Fletcher was no problem. And he described to Fletcher sitting by his Grandfather's bed how fine the airplane trip was going to be and how much Fletcher was going to like it in Los Angeles where they had the best temperature. Fletcher never said a word.

But after Louie went down to cook the breakfast Fletcher liked best, waffles and pork sausage, when he came back to Grandpa Larkin's bedroom with the tray, Fletcher was gone.

It was a shock to everyone in Crestview no matter how they felt about the Larkins, the spot that Fletch was in. The men organized to go out and find him. And next day when the police came through along with Army units, looking for missing persons, they scouted around for him too. But no one had a chance considering that Fletch knew the country around, all the meadows and shores, better than any of them. It was some time before Fletcher ever got found.

Personally, I caught up with him soon as I heard he'd disappeared. He was over at the culvert. He had an old hub cap balanced on top of a rock and he was spinning it, expecting I'd show up. I sat with him and after a while I tried to describe to him how much I liked his Grandfather, the one time I had a chance to meet him, and how bad I felt I'd never see him again.

"I guess it's just as well," said Fletch, "now the tree is gone. He sure liked that tree. He used to study it with his coffee every morning," Fletch told me, "the way you'd read a newspaper at breakfast."

Fletch went on for some time about his Grandfather, telling me of the different things they did together. It seemed a lot went on over at The Mansion. If nothing else, there was always an anniversary to celebrate with something special for dinner and especially for dessert. "Grandpa celebrated the day Babe Ruth hit his seven hundred and fourteenth home run and the day the Magna Carta was signed and the day Man O' War, some horse, won the Kentucky Derby. He always had a big day coming along to make a fuss over."

Just listening to Fletch I almost wished he'd let go for the comfort that'd bring him. But he never did. He'd stop, though, for long stretches and stare out of the arch of the culvert at the sunny day it was. Now and then he'd walk around outside to be by himself. I wasn't much use, far as thinking what to do that'd help.

"You heard about Los Angeles?" Fletch asked me. And when I told him I knew, he said, "Then you see why I had to get away from The Mansion. I can't let them ship me out to Los Angeles."

"I knew that's why you took off."

"It'd be different if I was someone like you. I mean wherever you fetch up you've got all that brain. But this is about the only place, around here, I'd ever make out."

"That's because here's where you belong," I reminded him.

He took a spin at his hub cap. "Being alone, I'm used to that. Though now when you think back on it, I wasn't so much alone with Grandpa the way he was. Anyway I can manage the alone part. It's leaving here," Fletch explained. "I can't."

"You're not going to," I promised. "We're not going to let anything like that happen."

He looked up with what was almost a smile. "After all the time we put in trying to keep you in Crestview, now I'm the one."

I was glad at least Fletch could get kind of a lift out of it. And actually, after Holy Hannah we Loverings did turn out to have no more problems left in Crestview. Everyone was thankful enough for the way Dad managed things during the storm.

And he was the one who stayed in charge for the next couple of days until it was easier for outside help to come in. Getting the streets so a car could roll again, and the water running and the sewers open and some of the worst houses patched, all that was organized by Dad until our home practically became GHQ for Crestview. No one took any notice by then of the bomb shelter. Seeing as how our family never used it during the storm, that was the same as if it weren't around any more. Everyone was our friend again.

And that went for the kids my age, as well. Their attitude turned back to the way it was before. When school finally did open up even Gardner Klein got hold of me. "You know that gasket we broke?" he asked.

"The X15?" I remembered.

"It's fixed."

"Well good."

"So any time you want to come back," Gardner suggested. And then he turned confused. "Except we had to travel some, you know, past Bagdad. Just to check it out, the gasket."

"Where'd you get to?"

"Johannesburg."

"But that's in South Africa?"

"Sort of."

"I thought you were headed for Europe."

"That was Pete Feddersen's fault," Gardner explained. "Somewhere along the line he made a wrong left turn. And then for two days we traveled on a map that was all a mistake."

"Well anyway," I said. "Thanks."

"Whenever you want," said Gardner. "We'll help you bring back the encyclopedias."

But by then I didn't have any time for the X15. Or for very much else besides Fletcher Larkin, keeping him out of sight so he didn't get sent off to Los Angeles.

The first days weren't too bad, long as Crestview and nearby had the luck to keep on being a disaster area. At the start the Army and the Red Cross had canteens spotted around serving meals for the homeless, so that Fletch just about had a choice of menus whenever he got hungry. Besides there were plenty of emergency cots set up one place or another, which Fletch didn't need.

Actually he couldn't have lived better. We found a forty-five-foot cruiser that slept eight about a hundred and fifty feet inland from the yacht club at Crest Cove. It was almost an apartment Fletch had to himself including a

refrigerator that was stocked with soft drinks. It was great to be aboard her for Fletcher especially at the start when he was getting over the worst of being without his Grandfather.

But pretty quick things started getting civilized and that made it rough. The cruiser was hauled back into the water, the canteens started to close up, and any homeless who came to sleep in a cot got checked by the police. That stopped Fletch.

We were forced into the culvert under the turnpike. I brought over my sleeping bag along with an extra blanket. And for food Fletch had to rely mostly on what I collected from the house a couple of times a day. Plus, we started to build a pair of walls in the center of the culvert out of dirt and rocks and old tires that Fletch could sleep between, so he'd be out of the wind. There was hardly enough time with all we had to do and when school started that made it rougher still.

Waiting for the bell every afternoon I didn't give much notice to what went on in school. It did seem that Miss Dokstra began asking me for a lot more than my share of whatever she wanted to hear. I answered her the best I could just to get it over with.

One of those days when the windows were still boarded and the class was under electric lights, she had me up to the blackboard three times. Twice was in arithmetic to transpose binary and duodecimal numbers and a third time in science to explain convection. I wrote the work out fast, so I could get back to my seat and down to the real problem, again, of what to do about Fletch.

But Dokstra wouldn't let up. She started in with me that

afternoon on the War of 1812, asking about the Embargo and Non-Intercourse Acts right down through the Hartford Convention and the end, the way it happened, of the Federalists. It became almost a private conversation and she wandered down from her chair to sit on Sommer's desk, next to mine.

"Very interesting," she smiled when I finally got through with it. "Welcome, Henry Three."

"Me? To where?"

"To the eighth grade. I've been waiting for the rest of you to show up and now, it looks, you're all here."

The class seemed to think that was a pretty funny remark. And it came to mind that I wasn't bothering to keep myself under control anymore. It didn't matter by then. What anyone thought about me wasn't important. Nothing mattered except to keep Fletch from getting shipped to L.A. I didn't try to explain to Miss Dokstra how Holy Hannah had changed things for me, for good.

I was about the only one in Crestview who did change, I mean in any permanent way. It was hard to believe. But I saw it happening all around me. Everyone went back to almost exactly what they were before. It was a mystery. They were all wonderful people, whatever peculiarities they had. Why they had to give up being so wonderful, I couldn't understand. One after another they all behaved as if they were waking up from a fine dream about themselves. And all they wanted was to forget it. None of what went on made sense.

Crestview shifted right into reverse once help came in from the outside, after we'd been working together for the first day or so. Soon as the ambulances showed up along with the plumbers' trucks and the carpenters the rush was to get your own private troubles repaired.

There wasn't a house didn't need a lot of work. With us a lot of the furniture we got when Dad made Vice-President was ruined and the wall on the left when you came into the living room lost its plaster. Our windows were gone. And it wasn't the money, since everyone was covered by insurance. It was the way you rated around town, how fast you got the job on your house underway. That started everyone remembering who they were to begin with.

Mrs. Feddersen showed up elegant again as a lady in a cigarette commercial. With her husband safe in the hospital, she didn't go on any more like a steam fitter. And Mrs. Andrews, she stopped being a sable. Mr. Driscoll came past looking like any banker on T.V. with a gray vest and a suspicious look and a cigar. It was the same with everyone else. And the only explanation I heard was, things were returning to normal.

Me, I couldn't return to normal if I wanted to. Not with Fletch up there in the culvert.

"How long do you think I'll have to stay here?" he asked me. "Out of sight."

"So they can't send you off to Los Angeles? I don't know, Fletch. But legal is when you're twenty-one. Then you can do what you want."

"That long?" The fingers of Fletcher's right hand worked against his pants. "More than seven years?"

I'd never stopped to think about it myself. "That's impossible," I told him.

"Who says so? Twenty-one minus almost fourteen is

practically seven. Seven years."

"Not the arithmetic. Hiding out that long is impossible."
I took another guess. "Maybe until you're sixteen is
enough."

"Well that's better," said Fletch. "Only two years. Especially I was thinking, if I had portable television. For
the winters. Summers I can handle. But we run a charge
account at Smith's Hardware in Bayside, if you wouldn't
mind picking up a portable television."

"Even so," I took a seat behind the dirt wall to get out
of the wind that blew through the tunnel. "You'll never
make it."

"It's not so bad here." Fletch sat on a bent-in twenty-
five gallon oil drum he used for an armchair. "Nothing's
as bad as Los Angeles."

"Can't you forget Los Angeles, Fletch? I gave you my
word, didn't I?" As if I'd ever let Fletcher Larkin out of
sight. When you came right down to it, most every good
thing that happened to me in Crestview was on account
of him.

Until Holy Hannah came along. And there was hardly
anything left of Holy Hannah, worth noticing, except my
father and me. We'd always be left, that was the promise I
had from Dad. He was starting to look like the last one
I could count on, my father, far as helping Fletch went.

Because from all I heard what Fletch needed to stay in
Crestview was a legal guardian, someone to stand up for
him. That was what I had to talk over with Dad, without
mentioning Larkin of course, since he was still a missing
person.

But once I got that idea and made it home one lunchtime, special, to put it up to Dad, I ran into trouble. The telephone was working again. And the first call in was from American Lock and Locomotive. It was Mr. Matthews himself on the wire.

"A reappraisal meeting," Dad said when he hung up. It meant he had to stop working on a drain over on Dorchester Avenue to get into the city. "Nothing I can do about it," he said, even though during Holy Hannah there was always something Dad could think up to do. Now he was even worried again.

"Plenty worried," he turned to Ma and me where we sat on the bathtub watching him shave. *Reappraisal* meant a meeting to shift things around where even a couple of vice-presidents could get demoted.

"Not you?" Ma asked.

"Not if I get in there," Dad smiled at her from out of his towel.

"If you don't mind my bringing up something," I suggested to Dad. "It'll only take a minute."

But there wasn't any time, they both pointed out, if Dad was going to make the 12:46. I got Dad to let me ride with him to the station except that didn't give us much chance either, rough as it was getting past the work in the streets and detouring where it was blocked off. Dad couldn't pay a lot of attention until we were on the station platform where there was a crew of carpenters hammering and sawing on the wrecked waiting room.

"We couldn't help Shep," I reminded my father.

"What's that? Oh, Shep Untermeyer."

"Because you said there was nothing we could do about

what was wrong with Holy Hannah or, you remember, wars."

"Of course, Hank." My father made sure the clasps were locked on his dispatch case. "I remember."

"What if there's something, though, that we can do?"

"About what?"

"To keep Holy Hannah from getting even worse."

"But the hurricane's finished," Dad stared at me. "What is this?"

"All I'm getting at, suppose there was someone in deep trouble, almost as bad off as Shep and I made a promise same as with Winner. You remember Winner?"

"The dog?"

"All I want to know is, how far would you be willing to go for us to keep the promise?"

"Us? You mean the family?"

"That's right. So we could become his legal guardian?"

"I see what you mean." From down the track the whistle sounded and Dad checked his watch. "You want me to talk to Mr. Untermeyer so we can take the dog and become Winner's legal owners." By now you could hear the far roar of the train. "Well, Henry, that's a good deal to think about and there's not much time."

"No Dad, not Winner. He's just an example, the dog is, of what I had in mind."

"Have a heart," Dad begged me. "I've got a bonfire burning in the office. Let me get in there and put it out. This is no place to work out examples."

"But it's simple enough."

"No it isn't, Henry. Besides it's a family matter. Why

don't you go back and take it up with your mother?"

"But it was you and me," I reminded him. "It was along the lines we were talking, Dad. About making it wonderful without anyone getting hurt. Instead of waiting for wars."

"Henry, please." Dad spotted the train down the track. "You'll simply have to lay off. Ma, she can handle this."

"Except it was you and me who went into it and I thought we two could work it out considering, you know, how we feel together."

"I know how we feel." Dad put his arm around me as the train pulled a shadow down the long platform and filled it with noise. He took me with him past the waiting room. "Don't get me wrong, Henry. I'll always feel that way. But we have to stop talking about wars and Holy Hannah. They're finished. We're back to living the way we were. Please give up, Henry."

"I can't. Not about this."

"But there's no time left. I'm sorry, son. You don't know what's facing me in the office."

"Well, as far as that goes," I gave up. "I know." I'd never forget what it was like for my Dad in his office, how different he was up there. "I guess it's too bad you got to go in."

"That's for sure." He gave my head a shove. "But what's a guy to do?"

I watched him make it up the train steps. He turned. He waved at me in a special way, as if to apologize for not having the chance to help me. But the look of him, with his hand stretched high, was like he was leaving on more than just a trip into town for a couple of hours. He yelled, "Goodbye Henry Three," as the train pulled out.

And that's the way I felt too, like he was taking off on an important trip someplace far away where he was going to stay for a long time. And I yelled, "Goodbye, Dad."

20

I KNEW YOU WOULDN'T WANT A BETTER FATHER, THE WAY he was deep down. The mystery was why it had to be down that deep, why the best part of him had to be so covered up. That's what I couldn't understand. And I guess I never will.

One thing was sure. Now that my father and the rest of them had gone back to worrying about their own private affairs, there didn't seem much chance anyone would be interested in helping Fletch.

I didn't know what to do. Every time I showed up during the next couple of days Fletch'd ask, "How're things?" That's all. He'd never put the question to me direct, whether I'd figured some way to get him out of the fix he was in. There was no doubt I was the one he depended on, me and my big percent. But there was no way to tell him how much tougher this was, his problem, than to think up an idea to stop wars.

"There's a couple of good angles I'm working on," was what I explained to him mostly. And Fletch would turn just as cheerful as I was trying to act. Both of us began to feel it was hopeless. He stopped asking me "How're things?" after a while. It got so we even quit mentioning Los Angeles or whether he could keep away from the place. The only question left, it seemed, was when?

So that each new day that he could still stick around, that was something to be thankful for. And lucky for us you wouldn't want a better early November than happened along. It seemed all the trees that were left tried to make up for the ones that were gone, the color they had. And after the hurricane it was Indian Summer, warm mostly.

We put in most afternoons with Fletch showing me the country around Crestview, swamps and backwoods and coves that no one seemed to know about. At least it was easy enough to keep out of the way of anyone who might mention Fletch to the police. We had a hot dog roast once with stuff I brought from the house and caught a striped bass, surf fishing off Cobbler's Creek, that gave us a chance for a fish fry.

A couple of times Fletch brought up about the Brotherhood of the Outer Reaches, how he was ready to initiate me if I wanted. But when I found out it took five days, that subject got dropped. There was no telling about days, how many were left. Otherwise we had a good time.

It didn't last. It turned cold, too bitter for living in a culvert. And then the bad news came that ended, as far as I could see, any interest there might ever be in

223

Crestview for anyone to help Fletcher Larkin.

It was the lawsuit that Grandfather Larkin had started so long ago. After all this time the last court that had the case passed out its judgement. And it was Mr. Larkin, the court said, who won. Soon as they heard the news everyone in Crestview was on the phone complaining to whoever would listen.

The fact is, the one who got beat in the case was the Crestview Land Corporation. They had to pay the Larkins damages amounting to hundreds of thousands of dollars. Unless the Larkins decided they wanted the land instead. In that event it was the families who would get paid the damages, for their houses and any money they lost.

Both ways, no one in Crestview was going to be out anything except everyone might have to move. And that was enough of a headache, the uncertainty of what might happen. Because by now, except for some lawyers and Fletch who was missing, there weren't any Larkins left to decide how things were going to be.

For the knot it tied everyone in, there wasn't much sympathy left around Crestview for the Larkins. Even for Fletch, wherever he was. I hated to break the news to him at the culvert. But the way Fletch took it, he turned happier than I'd seen him since the hurricane.

"Grandpa was right!" Fletch shook his fist at me. "How do you like the old gentleman? He always said he was going to win, and now he has!"

"Yes," I reminded him, "but it doesn't help you much, Fletch."

"Why not?" Fletch laughed. "Grandpa always wanted to see this land go back into potatoes and so do I!"

224

"Except there was always a couple of angles to work on, if we held out long enough. Like maybe we could get Crestview to sign a petition about you, or my father might stop being so tied up at the office. Something! But now it's all that tougher. Especially, if everyone has to move out so they can grow potatoes here again."

We sat in the windy culvert and Fletch nodded. "Well, I guess that's so."

I don't know why I had to spoil it for him, how happy he was. And then thinking it over, I was glad I did. It brought up an angle at least. One that might work. By the time Fletch was found, we'd figured it out to the place we were almost sure it would work.

It was my mother who found Fletch. That was on account of I moved him out of the weather into our Super Zero. It seemed safe enough considering no one ever showed up in the air raid shelter anymore. Except Ma did. Down she came and there was Fletcher Larkin, warm and comfortable, talking to me.

Ma was wearing a gray skirt with pleats and her hair in a bandanna and she stopped in the door at the sight of us. "Hello," was all she said.

"If you'd only give me a minute, Ma," I tried to tell her. "I can explain everything."

"How do you do, Mrs. Lovering," said Fletch.

"It's not how I do." Ma smiled at him. "You're the one, Fletcher Larkin, we've been worried about. And there you are! It's wonderful to see you. And praise be, you're all right."

"So far," said Fletch. "I guess I'm okay."

"We felt very bad about your grandfather," Ma told

225

Fletch. "And for you. It upset us all."

"Thanks for mentioning it ma'm," said Fletch.

"But where ever have you been? And food. Have you had enough to eat?"

"He's had me in hand," said Fletch. "Henry Three."

"You've had Fletcher down here all this time?" Ma asked me.

"Only since last night," said Fletch. "Unless you want to count the night before. He didn't bring me here until four in the morning."

"You, Henry? Four o'clock!"

"It wasn't he stayed up that late, Mrs. Lovering. Henry got up special. It didn't take more than a little while. So the sleep he lost didn't amount to anything."

"That's good," said Ma. "But the thing I don't get is all the cloak and dagger that's been going on. Why, you two? You could have told us, Henry. I'd have been glad to help."

"Would you, Ma?" I nodded at Fletch because that's what I described to him about my mother.

"I certainly appreciate that, Mrs. Lovering," Fletch said. "That you'd be glad to help. How?" he asked.

"Well," Ma counted it off on her fingers. "First, a good scrub. Then, clean clothes from top to bottom. Next, I sit you down to the best meal you ever had. And after a good night's sleep," Ma came to her thumb, "bright and early the next morning we call the police who've been looking for you."

"Police?" said Fletch.

"That's not the kind of help he needs," I tried to explain. "Call anybody and right there Fletch is on his way to Los Angeles."

"And the thing is, I don't want so much to go to Los Angeles," said Fletch. "I'd rather die."

"I'm sorry." Ma eyed the both of us. "I didn't know you felt that way, Fletcher. Is there anything can be done about it?"

"There sure is, Ma. As long as you're glad to help, you certainly can."

"Me?"

"He was coming up to see you, Fletch was, just as you walked in. Because the way it works out, it's not only us helping him. Fletch is our last chance too."

"For what?"

"To stay in Crestview. For him and for us both, to keep on living here." Ma sat down on the bunk, waiting to understand. "Go ahead," I looked at Fletch. "Didn't I tell you she'd be interested?"

Fletch felt at the collar of the sweatshirt he was wearing and pulled it down in front. "What I had in mind Mrs. Lovering was to make you sort of a proposition."

Ma gave a quick smile. "They're always interesting to listen to." She nodded for Fletch to go on.

"It seems what I need mostly," said Fletch, "is a legal guardian."

"And he wouldn't even consider anyone in Crestview," I told Ma. "Except us."

"So I wanted to ask you to be my mother," said Fletch.

It came as a startled sigh. "No!" Ma's hand went to her mouth to cut off whatever else she had in mind. She stared at Fletch. He sat down in the other bunk and looked at me.

227

"You can't say 'No' right off Ma."

"Maybe the whole idea," Fletch blinked. "The idea of me maybe, it don't appeal to her."

"She hasn't even heard it all. Give her a chance Fletch. You have to take things easy."

"That's true, Fletcher. This is very sudden." Ma stooped in front of Fletch with her heels curved out of their slippers, looking up into his face. "Understand me, it's not you, Fletcher. It's simply the suggestion, to be anyone's legal guardian. That's a terribly serious proposal."

"But you're ready to hear the rest of it Ma, and think about it, aren't you?"

"Of course I am." She patted Fletcher's knee.

"There!" I told him. "You won't find anyone fairer than my mother. Go ahead and give her the rest of it."

"Okay then." Fletch smiled. "If you'd like to take a seat, ma'm." Ma went back to where she'd been and you could see from the way she looked at Fletch how sympathetic she was to what he had in mind.

Fletch came to his feet again and fixed the sweatshirt. "First, of course, everyone gets tossed out of Crestview."

Ma swallowed. "What's that?"

"He's going to get rid of Crestview," I described. "You know, on account of the judgement. It's up to him, isn't it?"

"Well from all I hear," Ma felt at her throat, "I imagine it is, to some extent. But why would you want to do a thing like that, to a lovely place like Crestview?"

"It's just he doesn't think it's so lovely."

"Not the people so much," said Fletch. "During Holy Hannah they were all right to get along with maybe. But

I don't see why you have to wait for a high wind before you can be friends with somebody. Besides," Fletch reminded her, "it's what Grandpa wanted. To see this place back into potatoes again. Whatever he thought, that's good enough for me."

"Naturally." My mother's smile was worried. "Your grandfather."

"Except it's nothing we have to care about, Ma. We won't have to move, will we Fletch, long as we're your guardians?"

"No, of course not."

With her arms stiff behind her, Ma leaned back into the bunk. "So that's your proposition."

"That's it! We take Fletch into the family so he doesn't have to fly to Los Angeles. And him and us together, we stay behind when everyone else leaves."

"In the middle of a field," Ma stayed wide-eyed, "of potatoes?"

"Well anything like that is up to you, Mrs. Lovering. Where to live. You can stay right in this house, if that's where you want us."

"And the way we planned it," I told Ma. "Fletch and me would move down here in the bomb shelter. That'd be great for Sis. She's always yelling she wants a room of her own, without Lady. Now she can have mine."

"No, Fletcher," Ma shook her head at us. "It won't work."

"Then you can pick out any other house you think'd be better, Mrs. Lovering. They'll all be empty. The corner ones, they say, they're the most desirable. I guess they're bigger."

"Or Fletch even mentioned we could all go live in The Mansion. And they'd plow up the rest of Crestview the way it was before."

"I'm leaving it up to you, Mrs. Lovering," Fletch explained. "I'm just trying to make the best deal I can for you. And considering you can have any house you happen to choose, for free, doesn't that stack up as a pretty good business proposition? I mean, offhand?"

"But we have to be reasonable, Fletcher."

"That's all I want, ma'm."

"I mean what you're talking about." Ma rubbed her eyes with the palms of her hands and swept back the hair under her bandanna. "It's a family you're trying to put together. There's a lot more to it than real estate. It's the way you feel about each other. The love you share. What you mean together."

"I know." Fletch started to chisel a thumbnail clean. "On my side, it's pretty simple. I mean Henry Three, he's great. And your husband, he's as good a man as I've met around here. And you must be something yourself, to be teamed up with them. Besides the way you look just on your own. The thing is," he shrugged. "I don't know how to go into it exactly. I've never had too much experience talking to a mother."

"Fletch," Ma called and he looked up. "You do fine." She smiled at him.

"Well then, if you see what I mean, about the best I could hope for was to figure out a good deal you'd like. Because on my own, I can't look too much of a bargain right now."

"That's only the culvert," I explained to Ma. "Fletch

230

is very clean. He's always taking showers."

"I just like them better than baths," said Fletch.

"He's got good table manners. Wait'll you feed him," I promised Ma. "And you're neat, aren't you?"

"Grandpa used to think there could be some improvement. Especially my room."

"But there'd be the two of us," I pointed out to Ma. "Taking care of only one bomb shelter."

"All I can say is, Mrs. Lovering, I'd try. And that goes for school, too. Did you ever mention," he asked me, "how this was my second year in the eighth grade?"

"No use bringing that up. Long as we're going to be studying together."

"Except I don't want you to go into this ma'm, unless with your eyes open," said Fletch. "And I guess the cost side of it, that ought to be mentioned."

"Everyone's talking about how rich Fletch is," I reminded Ma.

"And if that's the case, for my food and rent along with laundry and incidentals, I won't cost you hardly anything." He looked over his hands and to hide them, I guess, he put them into his back pockets. "That's about all there is, ma'm, that I can remember. As far as telling you what to think about." Fletch sat down in the bunk to wait.

"What do you think?" I asked my mother.

"Henry! That's nonsense, to ask me now. This is going to take time."

I stood in front of her. "But you can tell him the trend, can't you? How your thoughts are going? So he'll know what to expect at least, while he's waiting down here."

"Down here?"

232

"Well sure, Ma. Where else? He's not going back to the culvert."

"But down here, Henry," Ma turned to Fletcher. "We'd be hiding someone, Fletcher, the authorities are looking for."

Fletch came to his feet, bewildered. "That's true, Mrs. Lovering. I certainly don't want to make any trouble for you. If that's how you feel." He stared at me as much to ask, what are we talking about? As long as Ma didn't want to take a little chance like that.

"You won't even hide him for a couple of hours? Until you think up an answer?"

"Hours? It'll take days and weeks to go into this, to talk it over with your father."

"But Dad said you're the one, Ma. It's a family matter. He left it up to you."

"You discussed this with Dad?"

"In a general way. And he said, take it up with your Ma. That makes it easier, doesn't it?"

"Not very."

"Even if you have to make up only your own mind? Let's say overnight, shouldn't that do it?"

"No Henry." The shake of Ma's head was final. "I'm afraid not."

"It's all right, Mrs. Lovering. You don't have to worry."

I turned to Fletch. He was standing with his hands in his back pockets again. And he had the same staring look to him that I saw the morning after his Grandfather died. Ma closed her eyes to Fletch as if she didn't want him to say any more.

"Even without the swap, Mrs. Lovering, it's no problem." Fletch took a deep breath and went on very quiet. "You don't have to make any deals with me. You can stay on in Crestview no matter what."

"Fletcher Larkin." My mother came to her feet. She put one arm around Fletch and he was almost as tall as she was. "Look at me, Fletcher." When he did, she said, "Please understand."

"I guess I do, Mrs. Lovering. I think I understand. All I want to get over is, you don't have to leave Crestview. I can see where I might be a little hard to take, even with a house thrown in. So you can forget about that." He rolled out of her arm as if he were getting past a basketball block. "When the rest of them go, you can stay. Just pick out any desirable address you want." Fletch reached into the bunk to take his windbreaker.

"Where are you going?" I asked him.

"Home. Or anyway over to The Mansion," said Fletch. "I thought I might take a shower."

"Are you crazy? One step through the door and they ship you to Los Angeles."

"No chance of that. Not until tomorrow morning, anyway."

"But give my mother some time, can't you?" I took his windbreaker. "To get her mind made up."

"It's made up," Fletch asked. "Isn't it, ma'm?"

Ma leaned against the post of the two tiered bunk and she studied the toes, pressed hard together, of her shiny black slippers. "Yes," she said.

I handed Fletch back his windbreaker.

The spring lock on the door of the bomb shelter is tricky. You have to give it an extra heavy turn to the left

234

before it unlatches. Fletch couldn't make it. I had to help him.

"So long," he said.

"Well, so long," I told him.

When he was gone, I turned. "Ma!" She looked up and her eyes had a high sparkle. "What's wrong? The way Fletch fixed it, at least we don't have anything to worry about."

"I know."

"Then what's wrong?"

"Well it's not every day, Henry Three, you get proposed to by someone who only wants you to be his mother."

She walked past me to the door and she handled the lock, with one turn of the wrist, by herself.

21

I BROKE A PLATE. THERE WAS NOTHING LEFT TO THINK about, except Fletch was gone. And nothing much else to do, except clean up. And the sink was filled with dishes left over from Fletcher's lunch. I washed them. There wasn't any problem with hot water because the house supply is piped into the shelter. In addition of course, the shelter has its own water storage and the two systems are controlled by a single cut-off valve. It was a neat set up, for anyone who might want to move in and live on their own.

I was drying the plate when it dropped. I stabbed and caught it about an inch from the floor. I didn't see why a plate should be saved, out of everything. I banged it against the faucet. It didn't even chip. And then with two hands I brought it down on the rounded white rim of the sink and it cracked, a clean and simple break, right in two.

I finished straightening the bed and rolled up the sleeping bag that Fletch had brought from the culvert, when the door opened. It was my big sister and Lady and they stood there as solemn as a couple of infield umpires.

"Ma says if there's nothing you're doing," Sis told me, "she'd like to see you."

"I'm done," I said. "I was coming up."

"Next year play school." Lady smiled. "That's what Ma says."

"Great," I told Lady. "I always knew you'd make it."

"What's wrong?" asked Sis.

"I'm okay."

"For Ma, though?"

"Nothing's wrong for Ma, far as I know."

"All of a sudden, no one wants to talk in this house," said Sis.

I picked up the sleeping bag that belonged on the top shelf of my closet. "As far as that goes, Sis, how're you doing? I mean with Warren Andrews and all?"

"Fine, thanks," she said. "But maybe you'd better get up there and see Ma."

The door to their bedroom, my mother and father's, was closed. I closed it again after I knocked and Ma told me to come in. She sat at her dressing table with her back to me and she put away a lipstick. Except the table had a skirt arrangement, blue and white, it was all glass with shining bottles and jars that had their own silver tops and mirrors that showed Ma looking at me from three different directions.

"What's that?" she nodded at what I was carrying.

"This? It's just my sleeping bag."

She turned and faced me. "Were you planning to go somewhere?"

"No ma'm." I described how Fletch had been using it over at the culvert. "I'll apologize if you want, for hiding Fletch out and bringing him over here. But I can't say I'm sorry, I don't think. The short time it amounted to."

"That's all right. And as long as you're not leaving home, why don't you put the bag down." Ma edged over and patted the cushion next to her. "Sit down, Henry."

There wasn't much room on the tiny stool, even though we sat tight as we could. "He's nice," Ma said. "Your friend Fletcher."

"Once you get to know him."

"Nice smile."

"And what you saw was even without a shower."

"I couldn't be sorrier for anyone. But you do understand, don't you Henry, what a serious obligation it is to take a fourteen-year-old boy into the family? It's an enormous responsibility."

"Yes ma'm."

"Then you realize there was nothing else I could do?"

"Well yes, if that's how you feel about it."

"And I hope you forgive me."

"Well, no ma'm. I don't think I can."

Ma's arm around me tightened. "Why can't you?"

"It's not so comfortable here," I pointed out. "Such a little stool. Do you mind if I sit on the rocker?"

It was a wooden rocker with a high ladder back that stood on the other side of the fireplace from Ma. It was old, not part of the furniture we got when Dad made

Vice-President. We'd had it in the family since even before Sis was born and Ma still used it sometimes to put Lady asleep. It was the best chair, far as I was concerned, wherever we lived.

Ma watched me pull my feet up into it. "Why can't you forgive me?"

"You told Fletch you'd think it over. That it might take days or maybe weeks. It didn't take more than a few minutes. You didn't think about it. Your mind was made up."

"I lied." Ma centered herself on the stool and the light that came from the dressing table behind traced her sharp and clear. "I tried to make it easier on Fletch to begin with. And then I saw it was just no use. To keep him waiting would only make it crueler."

"I understand." I shifted my weight and the rocker moved. There's a squeak you pick up about two thirds to a full swing. When the squeak came, I stopped. "If that's what you wanted to see me about," I stood up. "I guess I'd better put the bag away."

"Henry!" Ma's look kept me from moving. "This is your mother and you. We'd better get over this somehow. What happened with Fletch was wild, extraordinary. If I lied for a moment, it was only to get over a very bad moment. You know that we've always been truthful with each other, that you could always depend on anything I've told you." Ma waited till I sat down again. "Hasn't that always been the case?"

"No ma'm. I don't think so."

Her hands opened out. "But where Henry? How?"

"Crestview was always a big deal with us. That's what

you told me all the time. Now that it's fixed with Fletch so we can stay here, you switch. Now it's not so important, even if we have to move."

"But that doesn't make sense, child." Ma rocked too, on her stool. "We didn't come to New York City to live in the middle of a potato patch, did we?"

"Maybe not."

"Crestview isn't a place. It's people. Fine, successful people. They're the ones we came here to live with. If they have to move, we move too. To some other Crestview."

"Well, if that's what you want."

"It's not only me, what I want. This is for Sis and for Lady and you, for all of us. We're trying to give you a home where you can grow up into a world of real opportunity, where you can step into places your father had to fight all his life to reach. Isn't that what you want?"

"No ma'm."

"I'm talking about growing up."

"I'm not so interested."

"Do you know what you're saying?" my mother asked me.

"Well, it's just that when we had to see Mr. Matthews, Fletch thought I ought to take a chance growing up. I tried. I didn't like it too much. Not high up in those buildings where everyone's so afraid and worried. It was hard even to recognize your own father. I wouldn't want to grow up to be anything like that."

"Your father? After the magnificent job he's done for all of us? You don't know enough to judge him, Henry. It's my hope that you'll grow up to be something like your father."

"That's my hope, too."

"Then what are you trying to tell me?"

"Only that I'd like to be the same kind of man that Dad, you know, hides from everybody. The way he was in Holy Hannah. He was fine then, wasn't he?"

"Yes of course, that's one side of your father."

"I think it's the best side. Plus, it seems to make him the happiest. That's the way I'd want to be. Not the way Dad is up there on the seventy-sixth floor. That's not honest."

"Who's not honest? Your father?"

"It's just that no one is, not in Crestview, not so's you can notice. They're all about the same as me. The way I was, I mean, with my percent. I don't think that's so honest, how everyone goes around not letting on about themselves. Except during the hurricane, then all of them were honest. And a lot nicer too, to my mind anyway. Not that it makes much sense. I always expected people would hide what's wrong with them. Here they hide what's best. I don't know why."

Ma stared at me until I got up to the squeak again. "If you'd stay still a second," she took the bandanna off her head and tossed it on the dressing table. "Maybe I can tell you why."

I put my feet to the floor and braked to a stop. "It's not dishonest to live at something less than the best that's in you, Henry. Crestview is not a comic strip adventure day after day, with everyone trying to prove he's the greatest or the strongest or the bravest. Your father goes into business every morning not to show he's the best father or the best Marine Corps major. He goes in to do the job that's waiting for him, whatever it is. That's not dishonest. It's what you have to do to get along, to earn the security we need. Hurricanes and wars and violence, those are not the things we work at every day. That's simple enough to see, isn't it?"

"No, I don't think so."

"In Heaven's name, why not?"

"You were the one who told me, remember? How most of the men in Crestview did a lot of business with the Army and defense. If that's what they work at every day, it has to do with wars, doesn't it?"

"Yes of course." Ma combed her fingers through her hair. "But only in a remote way. It has nothing to do with violence and destruction. However we make our living, none of us want war."

"According to Dad they do. It's a secret."

"What is?"

"How a lot wouldn't mind if another war did come along, or a hurricane, so they can start living the best they can."

Ma studied me. "Your Dad told you that?"

"Yes ma'm."

Ma turned slowly to her mirrors to find a brush and with long strokes she curled the wave of her hair lighter and lighter in the glow of the dressing table. But she didn't look too pleased with the effect she got. I waited to hear if there was something else she had to tell me. She didn't speak.

"What I figured was," I stood up, "I'd better get that bag away. And then I thought I'd take off."

Ma quit brushing. "To go where?"

"Well the only thing I had a chance to say to Fletch was 'So long.' "

"You're going over to The Mansion?"

"You know, to tell him 'Goodbye.' " I headed for the sleeping bag that lay near the door. "If that's okay with you?"

"It's okay." Ma took my wrist as I passed her. "But not right now, Henry. Don't leave."

"Except there isn't much time for Fletch."

"Nor for us either, I'm afraid." Ma looked up at me. "When I think you used to be the best fellow I ever had, I don't seem to be doing so well anymore."

"I wouldn't say that."

"I would." Ma let go of me and went to sit in the rocker herself. She crossed her legs and with the toe of one slipper slowly tipped back and forth. "I've got a boy who won't forgive me, who can't really believe what I tell him. He doesn't want to grow up. He has the idea his father is dishonest. That his Dad and all the other men in town secretly want to go to war. I'd say he was in trouble. And I don't seem to be getting through to him. For a mother, I'm not much help."

"Me? It's not me, Ma, I'm not the one in trouble. It's Fletch. It's only that he has to leave in the morning. If it weren't for that, everything would be great."

"So I gather." Ma talked slowly, the way she rocked. "When Larkin's around it's great. Tell me, why?"

"You want me to tell you about Fletcher?" I sat down on the dressing table stool.

"Please."

"Well if you're interested I'd be glad to," I said. "The

thing is, Fletch is the best friend I ever had."

"And just what does that mean to you, Henry?"

"Just that we have some pretty good times together."

"You had a good time on the X15."

"Yes, but with Pete and those you never know when a gasket can break. Fletch isn't like that at all."

"What is he like?"

"Well it's the way you were mentioning. It's as if there were a hurricane every day or maybe a war here in Crestview but with no winds, Ma, and no bombs. That's the way it is with Fletch. It's just as honest with him one day as it is the next. The thing is, with Larkin you don't have to wait until it's dangerous, to do your best. You're always trying."

Ma nodded as she stopped moving in the rocker.

"For instance, you don't have to lie to Fletch. He even knew my percentage from the very beginning. He beat the truth out of me. It didn't make any difference to him how smart I was. Now it doesn't make any difference to me either, no matter who knows."

"I'm glad that's over with," said Ma.

"It's just when you got a best friend who doesn't mind, the others don't matter so much. And Fletch, he didn't even mind our shelter. You don't have to be ashamed with him or hide anything. As long as you're doing your best and you stand up for yourself. There was the fight we had. I never fought anybody harder. Fletch forced me into it. The best thinking I ever did was with him. You keep surprising yourself with Larkin, the things you can do. And that's why it's great with him, same as in a hurricane. Except with Fletcher Larkin it don't depend on some kid in the second grade who you can't even save."

"Shep Untermeyer?"

"That's right. No one has to get hurt. With Fletch, it's easy. You let yourself go just natural and it turns out happier than you thought it would be. Besides he's the best at flying a kite, Fletch is." I stopped and shifted a couple of bottles on my mother's dressing table. "I guess that's all there is to tell about him."

With her chin against a fist Ma leaned on the arm of the rocker. "It's clear you've found a little more to Fletcher Larkin than just a nice smile."

"It's only I've been a lot more in touch with him than you have, Ma. But seeing you were interested, I thought you ought to know." I waited but Ma just stared at me. "Does it make any difference? I mean with your mind? Or is it still made up?"

Ma rocked for a bit. "I'm afraid it is."

I reached from the stool and picked up the sleeping bag. "Then it looks like I'd better be leaving you, if that's all right."

"I don't see how I can keep you any longer," Ma nodded.

But I never did get the chance to say goodbye to Fletch. Outside The Mansion was crowded with extra long limousines. And inside, what I saw through the window, was crowded with men arguing over papers they gave Fletch to sign. I waited until considerably after dark but the meeting never did break up.

It was so late when I got home, the only light in our house was in my mother's bedroom. Ma was still in the rocker, what I saw through the window, with Dad walking back and forth smoking a cigarette.

I found a tray in my room with all my favorites, even coconut pie. So I sat down and had something to eat with nothing left to do except study the calendar over my desk. It has a real good color picture that wasn't much help, of a Boeing 707 Jet all striped in red, the kind of plane that doesn't take more than four and a half hours to fly non-stop from N. Y. to L. A.

22

It was a soft kiss on my right eye that woke me. "Henry," my mother whispered in the dark.

"What's up?"

The lamp went on and everything was hidden in the sudden light. Then they took shape beside the bed, my mother and father. They were all dressed.

"What's up? What time is it?"

"Almost five," said Dad.

"What are you doing up so early?"

Dad shook his head. "For us it's late."

"You haven't been to bed?" I could see they hadn't. Ma was wearing the same outfit as when I left her, the gray skirt with pleats. Pa had his shirt sleeves rolled up and he needed a shave. Around the eyes, both of them looked tired. "Is something wrong?"

"Nothing that can't be mended, Henry. I hope," said my mother. "Come, son, get dressed. We're going over to The Mansion."

"All of us?"

"Just you and your mother," said Dad. "This is her department."

"Why are we going over to The Mansion?"

"You'll find out," my mother pulled down the bed clothes. "It's no secret, Henry. But we've been through this so many times these past six or seven hours, I'd just as soon you hear about it with Fletcher."

By the time I came back from the bathroom they were stretched out on my bed, waiting. Dad had his arm around Ma and the two of them watched the ceiling. There was nothing you could figure out by the sight of them, what we were up to. And it was no use to keep on hoping any more. I dressed fast as I could.

Dad came with us and kissed Ma through the open window of the station wagon. "Good luck," he wished her.

There was plenty of night left when we got to The Mansion but the shadows were starting to bunch up and you could make out the torn roots of the big tree. When the door opened Louie stood in his heavy bathrobe and he was excited. "Please," he asked us. "What's happening? Hello," he said when he saw it was us, "can I help you?"

"We're sorry about the time it is," said Ma. "But we'd like to talk with Fletcher. Fletcher Larkin."

"Mr. Fletcher's asleep."

"I think he'd want to see us. I'm——."

"Henry Three's mamma." Louie led us into the downstairs library, the room Fletch and I used when we did our homework. Ma sat at the head of the long table and there was nothing for us to talk about, waiting for Fletch, except all the questions I was thinking. Long as Ma asked me, I waited with those.

Ma had a scarf over her hair tied in back and without lipstick she looked as if she were set to go to work around the house. It was the first time I ever saw her go out visiting like that. She was as pretty as ever though, far as I was concerned, and when I took a chance smiling at her instead of talking, she managed a tired smile back.

Fletch showed up in a long red robe that had his initials F. L. sewed fancy to the breast pocket. His hair was wet, I guess from splashing water on himself to wake up.

"Hi," he said.

"Hi," said Ma.

"You didn't have to come over to say goodbye," Fletch told us. "Not so early. I'm not leaving until day after tomorrow."

"My hope is," said Ma, "that you won't be leaving at all."

I sat up. In the long room the only noise was the ticking of a clock somewhere. From what Ma said, it was hard to understand what she had in mind. But the plain fact seemed to be that she was hoping, all of a sudden, for what Fletch and I had given up on. It was as if he suddenly came awake, the way Fletch took the remark. "Maybe," he asked Ma, "Louie could make you some coffee, if you'd like some?"

"I'd like some, thanks."

Fletch hurried back from the kitchen and sat at the table opposite me. Both of us watched Ma. She had a handkerchief out of her bag and she touched her nose, the way women do, without blowing it. She took a long breath. "I don't know if you can forgive me for yesterday afternoon?" she asked Fletch. "I'm afraid Henry can't."

"That's not it, Ma. I only said you didn't think about it."

"Well we've corrected that, Henry. Your father and I have spent the night thinking."

"About Fletch?"

"And about you."

"I don't see where there's anything for me," said Fletch, "to forgive you, Mrs. Lovering. I didn't have any call to take over your shelter just because I had a proposition you didn't care about."

"Maybe Ma cares about it now."

"No." Ma put the handkerchief away. "No propositions. I came to talk with you Fletcher about your need for a guardian. If that remains a possibility."

Fletch looked at me. I shrugged to show I didn't know what was up. "Well whether it's a possibility," said Fletch. "Sure it's a possibility. There was a raft of them over here last night, Grandpa's lawyers and those from the Crestview Company. Mostly it was about how they ought to make up my mind for me about Crestview. But Mr. Feeny and one of the others asked me if there was anyone in town I'd want for a guardian. I explained that wasn't the question."

"Does someone want him?" I pointed out to Ma. "That's the question."

"Not any more," said Ma. "Yesterday afternoon," she reminded Fletch, "You proposed to me. You asked me to be your mother."

"Yes ma'm."

"I accept."

Ma said it so quietly and she was so serious about it,

without any smile, you were afraid to believe what you heard. Fletcher's eyes went wide and he didn't move. With my hands on the table, I lifted slowly out of my chair until I couldn't go any further.

That's the way Louie found us when he came in wearing a white jacket over his bathrobe. He carried a large tray dripping a white cloth with silver pitchers and bowls along with an empty cup for Ma plus a couple of glasses of milk for Fletch and me, besides a plateful of coffee cake. Louie was a little startled as he left the room at how frozen still we were, with no one making a sound.

"Fletcher Larkin, we want you to come and stay with us." Ma reached across the table and touched Fletcher's hand. "And be part of our family."

"You do?"

"I do." And then it came, that high sprinkling laugh of my mother that tells when she's happiest. It left her a little helpless in her chair but not tired any longer, or serious. "I do," she repeated. "That's what you tell the preacher. And I guess this is just as solemn, this moment. I do, Fletcher. You're not alone any more. You don't have to be frightened any more of going to Los Angeles. Henry's Dad and I both want you very much to be our son."

I don't know what Fletch was up to but I had two arms around my mother and I bore down with a body-lock that started a scream. I'd given up kissing Ma years ago, in front of anyone except the family, but I didn't mind that Fletch was watching. He was part of the family anyway, starting now. There was no other way I could thank my mother for listening to me, for the way she listened to me all my life when I needed help the most. I ended up on her lap and Ma

251

pulled me to my feet. We turned to Fletch.

He was standing at his chair, lost, as if there were some mystery he couldn't figure out.

"Fletch!" I reached for him but he backed off. "You're saved."

"Leave Fletch be." Ma caught her breath. "Let Fletcher take this in his own good time."

"Thank you, Mrs. Lovering." He tried to look pleased. "I'm real glad you want me in the family."

"A little breakfast might help." Ma nodded us into our seats. "To get you used to the idea." She served us our milk and cake and poured herself coffee. I didn't know how Fletch could take it so quiet, the miracle it was. How he could eat! There wasn't much I could get down, with no one talking. "What's got into you?" I asked him. "What's the matter?"

"Why?" Fletch asked my mother.

"Why what?"

"Yesterday afternoon it seemed pretty definite. You know, that there was nothing doing. Now, this is like some of the dreams I've been having. And before it gets to be morning and anyone has to wake up I'd like to find out, why? I mean what your thought is, Mrs. Lovering. You already said you didn't want my proposition."

"No Fletcher, no proposition. We don't want any house, no matter how desirable. We want you. That's our only thought. We want you to put Los Angeles out of your mind and come live with us. Wherever and however we live, you'll be part of our home and our family. It's that simple. And it's up to you. I'll do everything I can to persuade you to come. But the whole thing's your decision, Fletcher, to say yes or no."

252

I never heard my mother talk that beautiful, so clear and slow and with such shining eyes. I never saw her ask for anything so hard.

"Well," Fletcher took a long swallow of milk, "that sounds pretty good," he looked at me. "Wouldn't you say?"

"It's everything," I pointed out, "I ever told you about my mother."

"I sure have to thank you, Mrs. Lovering." Fletch got a little more pleased. He smiled at Ma. "It certainly gives you lots to think over, doesn't it?"

"I know. It's a little overwhelming, for all of us. Breathe easy and just speak up, whatever comes to mind."

Fletch picked a couple of crumbs of coffee cake off the table and chewed on them. "No Los Angeles," he told himself. "I stay with you people. Where?" he asked Ma.

"In the house we live in right now. With you two in the bomb shelter, the way you planned. Or if everyone's obliged to leave Crestview, we'll find somewhere else as nice."

"But I told you," said Fletch. "You're staying. You're the only ones who can keep on here."

"I don't know if that would work out too well," Ma stirred her coffee. "To be the only ones in Crestview. There'd be no school. No train stop. No neighbors. Instead of living in the middle of all those potatoes, I think we ought to have our home in a more normal kind of community, don't you?"

"Well if that's what you think, I don't know." Fletch finished his milk. "I had a different idea." He twisted the glass on the table to study the white design that was left. "Same as my grandfather. His idea was to get rid of everybody."

"Of course. I know how loyal you are to your grand-

254

father. If that was his wish and it's yours, and the lawyers and the courts and whoever else has to decide, then go ahead. What's that got to do with how much we want you in the family?"

"But my idea was to live here in Crestview, sort of, on our own."

"That's simply not practical. And the point is, we didn't come over here to discuss what's going to happen to Crestview. But to you, Fletcher. You're the one we want to hold on to, if you'd only say yes. The business of Crestview, that can all be taken care of later in any way that you wish."

"I see." Fletch examined his glass. "Maybe it's not practical." He tilted his head way back to get a last drop of milk. "Except, I don't know." He shook his head and stayed worried.

"What are you suspicious about?" I asked him. "This is better than anything we imagined. There isn't even any deal here you have to think over. Ma's just asking you straight out."

"With no ifs, ands or buts. With no strings attached. Please, Fletcher?"

"Look ma'm, I don't mean for you to beg so much." Fletcher looked back and forth along the table like there was something he'd lost. "I'd feel better about this if we did have a deal. Where I gave you one thing and you gave me another. I could understand that. But this way."

"Can't you conceive that someone might want you around," Ma smiled at him, "just on your own? With nothing else thrown in?"

"No ma'm. The truth is, no one ever has. Except the Old Man, Grandpa. And Henry, maybe. But the way you talked yesterday afternoon about putting a family together, you mentioned all the feeling that went into it. You even made the remark, you know, about love. Well I don't see how anything like that can come up so sudden, practically overnight."

"To be sure Fletcher, you're right." With both hands around her cup and elbows on the table, Ma drank her coffee. Her eyes closed and from the way she loosened in her chair she seemed tired again. "In all honesty, we don't love you."

"Well that stands to reason, ma'm."

"We admire and respect you. We think you're a fine young man, and one day I'm sure we will love you. But there's something else almost as important that goes into making a family. And that something we do feel about you, Fletcher. We need you. Let me make it very clear, we need you."

Ma didn't go on. And there was no answer I had for the look Fletch gave me. We waited while the far off clock ticked, while Ma poured herself more coffee and added cream to it from a high polished pitcher and went to searching with a pair of tongs in the silver sugar bowl. We waited while she stirred the coffee. "It creeps up on you, doesn't it?" Ma smiled at us. "How endlessly weary you can get."

Carefully Ma put the coffee to one side and she never drank it. "But late as it is, you certainly deserve some explanation, Fletcher. And the fact is, yesterday afternoon I came to a very sharp turn in the road. The one you and I have been going along, Henry."

"When we talked?"

Ma nodded. "You want to make the turn that we've reached and start out adventuring. I'm afraid I can't go with you. Not to find what you're looking for."

"What are you looking for?" Fletcher asked me.

"Me? I don't know," I said.

"Yes you do. I'd say you were looking for yourself, Henry. For the way you're going to be at your very best and your most honest. I don't think there's any greater adventure. I'm glad to see you go, even though it's an effort for me to say that. Because it's no trip that a mother can take. And your Dad? Well that's what we talked about for so long last night, the way things are with your father."

"You mean at the office, how tied up he is?"

"Dad and I did you all right, at least I hope so, as long as it was comforting you needed and security. But the adventure he's on now, Fletcher, there's no one around our house who can travel with Henry Three. You though, from all I gather, you're going the same way. I think the two of you together can make it. If you want to come with us and try. So there it is Fletcher, that's all it is. My boy's leaving me and I want someone to go with him. We need you just as much as you need us. That's kind of a swap, isn't it? Something you can understand."

"Yes, Mrs. Lovering."

"That's why I say the place isn't important. Whether it's here in Crestview and you're underground, down there in the shelter. Or it's somewhere else. Wherever it is you two will have the chance you want to find a life of your own, no matter how different it might be from the rest of us."

Ma piled her fists on the table, one on the other, and rested her forehead on top. "At least you'll get the best chance a mother can give her son." She looked up, shifting her chin to the fists on the table. "Or is it, sons?"

257

The look there was between them held until Fletcher smiled too. "Yes, Mrs. Lovering," said Fletch but in a high voice that came to a sudden stop without covering, the way it sounded, all he had to say.

"What does that mean?" I wanted to know.

"Just that your mother's been asking me a question. And all I'm trying to tell you is, yes."

"That you'll come be with us?"

"That's right. Long as you want me, I'd like to say yes."

No one laughed. No one even smiled anymore. I thought that when this time would ever come, when it was settled for Fletch and me both, there'd be an explosion. That we'd toss books, break furniture. It wasn't like that. It was quiet. You heard the clock again. It was coming on to morning again, and the windows turning gray. It was tired. It was no time for a celebration.

Ma pushed herself straight in her chair. "I'm grateful," she said. "Fletcher, I'm very grateful."

"You're the one, Mrs. Lovering, who ought to get thanked."

"We're going to do our best to make you happy."

"I'll try too. As far as being neat goes, Mrs. Lovering, and the way I am around the house, wherever we live."

"You won't regret too much not being on a potato farm?"

"Well, potatoes. There's a lot has to get decided before we can grow any potatoes in Crestview."

"Whatever happens Fletcher, we'll keep up The Mansion, won't we? Maybe one day you'd like to come back and live here."

"I think so, Mrs. Lovering. The thing about The Mansion is, it suits me."

"It's a lovely house." Ma bent back in her chair and studied the lamp overhead, working her shoulders to ease them, I guess, from how cramped she felt. "And it's a lovely morning. You've made me a happy woman, Fletcher Larkin."

"And so have you. I mean, Mrs. Lovering, I'm certainly happy."

"What do you keep calling her Mrs. Lovering for?" I asked Fletch.

"What else should I call her?"

"Ma," I made the suggestion.

23

SO THAT AT THE END IT WASN'T FLETCH ANYMORE OR US Loverings. We weren't the problem. It was Crestview, what to do about Crestview. And Fletch's mind was made up.

"I'd just as soon get rid of the place," Fletch told us at the table that night, the first time we all sat down to dinner. "Once and for all."

"Then that's it," Dad passed a plate of the roast beef he was carving. "You're ·the one chiefly concerned." He described how the legal side worked. Fletch was an 'infant heir' according to law who was looked after by a special court, a Surrogate's court that had to judge what was best for him. "Anything you have in mind though, the court will go along with," Dad explained to Fletch, "unless the judge thinks it's against your own best interest. I don't see what you decide about Crestview, either way, would conflict with your own best interests."

"So all he has to do is speak up," I checked with Dad, "and Crestview's done for," I pointed out to Fletch.

"That's fine with me," Fletch took the cranberry relish Ma held across the table. "If it's okay, I mean, with you people."

"No sir," Dad put down his knife. "This is up to you, Fletcher, and your attorneys and the court. This family is not going to influence you one way or the other."

"Our only wish is for you to be happy," said Ma.

"Well, when it comes to happy," Fletch worried through the mouthful he was chewing, "I'm happy. Thanks to you, Mrs. Lovering and you, sir, I don't see how I could be much happier."

"I'm happy," said Lady. She had her own way of speaking Fletcher's name, on account of Ma was always correcting her when she said runnin' or comin' or goin'. "Fletcher Larking has the best ears."

After we all agreed with Lady, Fletch kept on, anxious. "But supposing I do get rid of Crestview, where'll you go? That's to say all of us, where'll we go?"

"Larkshaven is my vote," said Sis. "It's the only place around has its own community discotheque."

Ma suggested, "Far Harbor. We're almost ready for that bracket don't you think?"

Dad nodded. "Or this new development, Huntsborough. It's two stations closer in."

"But all those places, aren't they the same as Crestview?" asked Fletch.

"Just about," Dad agreed.

"Then what's there to decide?" Fletch wanted to know.

It was after dinner and we were down in the shelter, putting our stuff away. "If we just end up in some other Crestview?"

"At least you'll get rid of this one. You'll be the first kid in history, I ever heard of, who got back at a town by wiping it out."

"I'm not looking to get back at anybody," said Fletch. "That's not it. It's only the old man, my grandfather, I always wanted to go along with his idea."

"Well no one's stopping you, not now."

"Except what good'll it do?"

"Then why can't you be like my mother mentioned, Fletch, just happy? You're saved from L. A., aren't you? And once Dad gets the papers signed, you'll be a full fledged member of the family. The thing is, we've always lived in places like this. You'll get used to it."

"Who wants to? Now I got the chance, it's Crestview I want to get settled about. If you'd only give me a hand, Hank. Some idea what to do?"

"No sir. You heard my Dad, we're not supposed to influence you one way or another."

"But you got to help." Fletch dropped an armful of socks into his drawer and banged it shut. "Look, are you ready to get initiated into the True Brotherhood of the Outer Reaches?"

"Anytime."

"Okay. Once you're in that's who I'm going to put it up to. Let the Brotherhood decide about Crestview."

It took me five days to get initiated and I just barely survived. The first four days were preliminary and on each one I had to surrender something else. Like the first day I had to give up hearing, with my ears plugged. And the next, seeing, with a blindfold. On the third I stopped talking, with my mouth taped. And last, I had to give up eating for one whole day.

My condition, the worse it got, attracted a lot of attention. Ma was bewildered, even though she expected life might be different for us down in the shelter. Miss Dokstra was patient, when Fletch tried to explain about the virus spreading through my eyes, ears, nose and throat. There wasn't any comment from the rest of the class as long as it was Fletch leading me around when I was blind, or listening and talking for me when I was deaf and dumb. Most everyone was respectful of Fletch, now they knew he was the one the future of Crestview depended on.

Starved as I was from not eating that last day, then is when the real initiation began. I spent the night in a tree watching for a sign that Fletch promised would come out of the east. It turned out to be a cardboard sign that showed up at daybreak hanging on to a branch overhead. It told me to get back to the shelter where it was pitch black and Fletch jumped me from behind. He stretched me out on a plank that was balanced across a couple of chairs, bawling, "Farewell to the Life that Was!"

I was supposed to be laid out for a corpse. Instead I kept falling off, dozing, to the linoleum covered cement floor three feet below. When he did leave me up, Fletch held me by the back of the skull neck deep in salt water until I was a quarter breath from drowning. "All Hail," he let me go, "All Hail to the Life that Is!"

Two lights waved up, a pair of candles that showed Fletch in an old raccoon coat he'd brought from The Mansion. He read out of a ledger, where his grandfather had the initiation written out, that I had a Feast coming. Even though it was only the Light of Wisdom, no more than a drip of wax off the lit candle, and the Blood of a Wild Boar which was a half can of tomato juice, and a Pearl of the Oldest Sea which was a hard-boiled egg, by then anything to eat was welcome.

"Let there Now be Revealed the Secret of Our Order." Fletch pulled down a dish towel that hung on the wall. "Behold that Great and Marvellous Mystery of Perfect Revelation, the Cut Broom Stalk." And that's all it was tied to a nail, just a couple of straws out of a kitchen broom.

"Virtutem Suam Augere." Fletch yelled out the Latin that was in the ledger. "Grow With Courage." He banged me with his elbow, to follow along.

"Virtutem Suam Augere," I let go. "Grow With Courage."

Fletch could've been a conductor announcing the next station. "You have Arrived Within Thy Everlasting Home Within the True Brotherhood of the Outer Reaches." He banged me again. "You are my Brother."

"You are my Brother," I yelled back.

"How do you feel?" he asked me, his voice normal again except for sounding a little hoarse.

"How do I feel? Do you mean it's all over?"

"Practically."

"I don't know, how do you feel?"

"I wasn't the one took the beating."

"I mean, you just said we were Brothers."

"From now on."

"How do you feel about that?"

264

"Fine." Fletch had on his big smile and he hung the raccoon coat over one of the new hooks we'd put up, trying to be as neat as he promised my mother.

"What I'm asking, do you feel like anyone's brother?"

Fletch thought it over. "Not particularly."

"Me neither."

"Except how would we know what a brother feels like. You and me, we've never had one before."

"I just thought there'd be some change would come over us, all the trouble we went to."

"You belong to the True Brotherhood of the Outer Reaches, Hank, isn't that enough? You're home. The way it says in the book, you're in thy everlasting home. You have to get used to the idea. Give it some time."

"I don't see where it makes so much difference to you."

"In what connection?"

"There's Crestview. If thy everlasting home amounted to anything, for real, then you wouldn't be worrying about this place."

"Maybe you got something there." Fletch leaned against the stove where the candles flickered across the white enamel top. "You know, it only goes to show."

"What?"

"I told you I was going to leave it up to the Brotherhood, didn't I, what to decide about Crestview? And now you have."

"Me?"

"It's the way you just put it, Crestview's nothing to worry about. Far as having a home, any real home, we don't belong to Crestview. No matter where we live, what we

266

belong to is the Brotherhood we're in together. You're absolutely right."

"I'm glad of that." It was a pleasure to watch Fletch, how happy he was.

"It settles the whole problem. We might as well stay right where we are."

"Here, at least we couldn't have a better survival unit to live in. If you don't mind, that is, crossing up your grandfather."

"I've been putting my mind to Grandpa. Long as I have to stay in some kind of Crestview, he'd just as soon see a Larkin stick around, don't you think, where there's always been one?"

"No question. And besides look at the bother it gets rid of, not having to move."

"That's something I figured Ma would appreciate."

"Ma?"

"Wouldn't she?"

"But Fletch," I grabbed him. "What are you talking about? You never spoke of my mother as anything but Mrs. Lovering. Now you're calling her Ma."

Fletch stopped yelling. "So help me," he whispered. "That's right."

We held each other and we looked around at the slow moving shadows of the bomb shelter. "Maybe something has happened," I stayed quiet as Fletch. "If she comes out Ma, if that's the way you got her in mind, you know what that means?" Wide eyed, Fletch waited to hear. "The initiation took. We're changed somehow. We're brothers. I mean for good."

"It worked."

"It had to. If we got the same Ma, we got to be brothers."

"The thing is, it worked."

And then it even felt like we were brothers holding on to each other down there in the small light of the candles. Brothers are bigger than most and braver, the way it feels. They stand straight and proud and thankful that they'll never be alone again. They're too filled up for any little room like a bomb shelter. "Let's get out of here," I asked Fletch. "Let's go tell her."

"Ma?" Fletch agreed, "wait'll she hears."

But there was one last thing. I had to register. The ledger had to be signed with a new and secret name, not just Henry Three. The name Fletch took belonged to one of his uncles. I copied the name of another uncle he had. Then we had to form a circle and say out loud who we were.

We put a hand on each other's shoulder and Fletch said, "I am Andreus."

And for anyone's who's interested in what happened next I said, "I am Michaelus," and then we went up into the morning.